WALL STREET CHRISTMAS

WALL STREET
Christmas

ROBERT GAMBEE

W. W. Norton & Company
NEW YORK · LONDON

For my grandfather—
who came to Wall Street a hundred years ago
and spent the rest of his life there.

Library of Congress Cataloging in Publication Data
Gambee, Robert
Wall Street Christmas
Includes index.
1. Wall Street—Financial Community of New York
   —Description—Views
   —History
   —Securities firms
   —Banks
   —Exchanges
GT4986.A2N484 1990
394.2'68282'097471–dc20
89-39138
CIP

Printed in Japan by Dai Nippon Printing Company Ltd.
Designed by Jacqueline Schuman
Production supervised by Tsuguo Tada

Wall Street and Trinity Church

(Frontispiece) At the head of Wall Street, past the Doric columns of Federal Hall, J.P. Morgan's pyramid, and the Art Deco lobby of Irving Trust, is Trinity Church. Sitting astride the nation's most important street, Trinity still commands a presence even when surrounded by taller structures. When completed in 1846, its tower made it the Empire State Building of its time—the tallest structure in New York, symbolizing the entire city. Even today it is powerful, making a strong Gothic Revival statement as it stands boldly at the front of the church.

The Street's name derives from the Dutch *de Waal*, a wall of planks and beams erected in 1653 across the island to protect the community from surprise attacks by Indians and the British. However, the attack did not come until 1664 and it was by sea; the wall never really served its purpose.

Excerpts from the following works have been reprinted by permission.
Here Is New York © 1949 by E.B. White, reprinted by permission of Harper & Row, Publishers, Inc.
Manhattan Transfer by John Dos Passos © 1953 by Elizabeth H. Dos Passos (Executrix)
Leaves of Grass by Walt Whitman © 1900 by David McKay
American Notes by Charles Dickens © 1891 by Dodd Mead & Co.

CONTENTS

Special Acknowledgements

For assistance with historical information:
John Eckelberry
John Morris
Stephen Norman
Charles Parnow
Richard Urfer
Joseph Warner

For assistance with architectural information:
Paul Goldberger
Christopher Gray
Henry Moscow
Donald Reynolds
Norval White
Elliot Willensky

For editorial assistance:
Brian Cooper
Starling Lawrence
Marie Miller
Candace Watt

Photographic Books by Robert Gambee
Nantucket Island in Black & White (*Introduction by Nathaniel Benchley*)
Manhattan Seascape: Waterside Views Around New York
Exeter Impressions (*Introduction by Nathaniel Benchley*)
Nantucket Island in Color
Princeton in Color (*Introduction by Robert Goheen*)
Wall Street Christmas

INTRODUCTION

Wall Street—the most famous address in America. Main Street and State Street may be more common; there is only one Wall Street. It summarizes in two words the greatest financial center in the world, whose stock and bond markets exceed all others. It is a short street that begins at the steps of a church and ends in a river, and yet it is a street where more fortunes have been made (and lost) than any other.

Of the many faces of Wall Street, few are as joyous and predictable as its Christmas season. The large trees in front of the Stock Exchange and at Bowling Green, the magnificent lobby decorations, even the trees stuck in the masts of the ships at the South Street Seaport have a gentle glow that is impossible to ignore.

At first blush, "a Wall Street Christmas" appears to be a contradiction in terms. But underneath the high-speed tape, the computerized arbitrage and the trades of synthetic instruments, there exists a feeling in each of us that wants to reach out and be touched by others. It is a feeling that often lingers year-round and, for most people, bursts forth during the year-end holidays.

After the last trades are done, the confirmations processed and the floors of the exchanges swept up by the night crew—after the phones stop ringing and the video screens are motionless—then the celebration of Christmas begins. Whether it's Christmas or Season's Greetings, the spirit that permeates every city and hamlet in the country also permeates Wall Street as these photographs hopefully will show. Wall Street becomes a democracy again where everyone, from clerk to President, is on an equal footing—at least during the annual Christmas party. Pageants take place at Trinity Church, the pace slows and the entire holiday period offers a wonderful time to shop, lunch with colleagues, exchange Christmas cards and to realize that the friendships formed over the years are among one's most treasured assets. This book is not so much about the companies with majestic facilities but of companies whose citizens have all contributed in one way or another to make this the great financial center it is.

The captions I have written are designed to recall some of the great achievements of Wall Street's past. Many of the records set today make the accomplishments of yesterday pale by comparison, and yet each should be savored in its own context. In the 1960s were the IPOs, unit offerings and convertibles; REITS and sale/leasebacks dominated the 1970s (which also saw the end of fixed-rate commissions); then came Rule 415, the CMOs, LBOs and pac-man defenses. Going public, going private, restructuring and recapitalizing—some beneficial and some not, but there is always a willingness to take things apart, to analyze and to change.

There were seventeen investment banking firms identified by the Securities & Exchange Commission in 1948 as allegedly forming a conspiracy to restrain and monopolize the new issues market. The government lost its case. Judge Harold Medina of the Southern District Court of New York summarized the histories and present-day activities of these firms in his famous opinion, written in 1953. The order in which he selected them is as follows, and it is interesting to note that out of seventeen, only the names of eight exist today:

Morgan Stanley & Co.
Kuhn, Loeb & Co.   Smith, Barney & Co.   Lehman Brothers
Glore, Forgan & Co.   Kidder Peabody & Co.   Goldman, Sachs & Co.
White, Weld & Co.   Eastman, Dillon & Co.   Drexel & Co.
The First Boston Corporation   Dillon, Read & Co. Inc.
Blyth & Co. Inc.   Harriman Ripley & Co. Incorporated
Stone & Webster Securities Corporation
Harris Hall & Company Incorporated   Union Securities Corporation

One of the saddest discoveries in doing this book was *not* the degree of change, for without change the industry would atrophy, but the degree of focus only on today's transactions. There is little regard for the future and almost no recall of the past. Driven by the high volume of present events, we often forget some of the great institutions and developments that have played an integral part in making Wall Street the financial center that it is. One of the purposes of this book is to tell some of these stories. The tombstone that appears below is a tribute to the many people who worked for firms—some great (and some not-so-great), all of which have disappeared in the past twenty years. Not a name in this syndicate survives.

Thank heaven for starters! In my quest for information about the former whereabouts of various institutions, I found the old, seasoned elevator starters to be most helpful. The starter at 115 Broadway helped me locate one of the great finds of this book, the old Lawyers' Club (which has never been photographed under its new ownership). The starter at 120 Broadway guided me to the former Bankers' Club facilities. The starter at 40 Wall Street told me about a former tenant, "Cube Loeb", and the one at 26 Broadway helped me find John D. Rockefeller's old Standard Oil Company office.

I claim no credit for the photographs which I took for this book or for the historical information I have gathered. The views, the images, the ideas and the facts were all presented to me as the project unfolded. Throughout this journey I did not always know where I was going. I simply followed the thoughts as they came; the results must speak for themselves.

In researching the information for the captions, I was struck by the wealth of history that I had not been aware of. Take Broad Street, for example. Its unusual width is due to its origins as a canal—"The Gentlemen's Canal," which extended up to where Dow Jones used to be. In fact, the Long Island Ferry tied up in front of where Schrafft's (now Hoolihan's) once was—a famous restaurant that until 1970 did not permit women into its downstairs men's grill.

At the head of Broad Street is the famous Morgan bank, a structure which "J.P." could have designed to be the largest in New York, with a grand entrance and a multitude of leading brokerage and law firms as his tenants. He chose the opposite. Barely four stories in height, it was the epitome of understated elegance on one of the most expensive parcels of land in the country. Across the street is the majestically columned New York Stock Exchange. And yet if one visually removes the columns and pediment, it becomes a fairly modest structure which has been overcome with grand designs. To its credit, the Exchange remained open during the difficult period of October 1987, a far cry from 1914, when it closed for four months (along with major European exchanges) at the beginning of World War I.

Further down Broad Street, past the site of the old Curb Exchange (now called the AMEX) is an historic treasure. Behind its cheap dress shop image is the history of a magnificent Greek Revival temple at 37-41 Broad, which was built as the headquarters of Lee Higginson Corporation, one of the greatest investment banking firms of the first quarter of this century. Across the street at 60 Broad Street is the infamous Drexel Burnham Lambert. The ground floor is occupied by Dresdner Bank, directly opposite its staunch competitor, Commerzbank. Of all the locations in New York, they chose to square off against each other on Broad Street. At 90 Broad was Stone & Webster Securities Corp., a major-bracket underwriter set up by its engineering parent to capture some investment banking business from its

Not a name in this tombstone survives today.

rapidly growing pipeline utility clients. Goldman Sachs occupies 85 Broad, a site that originally was to be the world headquarters of its competitor, Lehman Brothers. It is also the site where Captain Adriaen Block launched the *Onrust*, the first sailing vessel built in America. He and his crew were the first settlers in Nieu Amsterdam in 1613.

Across from Goldman Sachs is the old American Bank Note Building at the corner of Beaver Street—formerly another canal. Fraunces Tavern sits at the intersection of Pearl and Broad Streets. This is where Washington spent his executive down time in the years before he was inaugurated as President a few blocks up the street. Pearl Street was once the city's outer extremity. Its name derives from the oyster shells with which it was originally paved. At the end of Broad Street, across from the Municipal Ferry Piers, is the present headquarters of Salomon Brothers, whose trading floor was simply the largest in the world when it was completed in 1970.

The foregoing is a sampling of what one discovers in walking through the pages of this book. Whether it's Wall Street or Broad, the World Financial Center or even Sixth Avenue, this is a community like no other. It celebrates its accomplishments and bemoans its failures as the tide rises and falls, yet nothing equals its Christmas spirit which returns unceasingly every year. Come celebrate this year-end event in the greatest financial center of the world.

The City

"Wall Street" is not just a street. It is an area as well as a state of mind. It is the financial district of New York, a city within a city, and thus may be considered the same way as the financial district in London—simply "the City."

Christmas on Wall Street begins at this famous intersection dominated by the New York Stock Exchange, J.P. Morgan & Co., and the Federal Hall National Memorial. The Exchange building was designed by George Post and completed in 1903. The massive facade of colossal Corinthian columns and pediment, anchored by a two-story podium, is designed to impart strength and prominence to a building of otherwise modest size. It remains a potent symbol of the most important financial institution in this country.

THE CITY

The American Surety Company Building

(Above) Clearly, one of the loveliest buildings downtown is 100 Broadway, built in 1895 and extended in 1921. It is presently the home of the Bank of Tokyo. This was one of the first structures in New York to use non-supporting walls. Upon its completion, it was the tallest building in the world, such that the National Weather Bureau located its office here.

Trinity Churchyard

(Opposite) Through the light snow can be seen the American Stock Exchange (behind the tree), New York University's Graduate School of Business Administration, and the Bankers Trust Plaza building.

Many young runners, as the messengers were once called, have unwittingly been sent to make deliveries to the venerable firm at 103 Broadway—Church & Graves.

This section of Broadway was originally called by the British Church Walk, and the first two streets north of the wall were originally King and Queen Streets, renamed Pine and Cedar, respectively, after the war.

The New York Stock Exchange

Completed in 1903, this building was originally going to have tenants on the upper floors. But the governors felt such a move was unseemly because it placed the Exchange in the role of a dowager of reduced circumstances forced to rent rooms. J.P. Morgan had the same attitude when he built 23 Wall Street. There was to be no space available for other tenants.

Architect George Post was asked to design a commercial palace in keeping with the prestige of the organization. He accomplished this with a facade of 52-foot-high marble columns whose height gave the building a stately appearance.

Three of Wall Street's best addresses

A view of 120 Broadway, 100 Broadway, and Two Wall Street. These are buildings known as much for their current tenants—such as Doremus & Co. at 120, Bank of Tokyo at 100, and Banco Portugues at Two Wall—as for their previous tenants: Equitable Life, American Surety, First Boston, and Morgan Stanley. The last occupied the same offices at Two Wall Street from the inception of the firm in 1935 until 1967. It also might be said that Morgan Stanley ruled the corporate bond market from this location. It was the only firm to print "red herrings" with the complete syndicate already listed, and the only firm to send its own associates to Washington to file offerings with the Securities and Exchange Commission— such a sacred mission not being trusted to outside counsel. Well into the 1960s, the associates were instructed to travel by overnight train as it was more reliable than the air shuttle.

Christmas at Bowling Green

The tree was donated to Wall Street by the Canadians and sits on the site where Governor Peter Minuet of the Dutch East India Company's Nieu Amsterdam made the strategic purchase of Manhattan from the Canarsie Indians in 1626 for trading goods valued at sixty guilders, or approximately twenty-four dollars.

(Left) The vicissitudes of Wall Street are illustrated by the histories of its firms. Take E.F. Hutton & Co., for example. During the 1960s, it occupied the forty-second floor of One Chase Manhattan Plaza and was always confused with W.E. Hutton & Co. In the 1970s, the latter disappeared without a trace and E.F. moved into its *own* build-

ing at One Battery Park Plaza (seen in the photograph directly behind the U.S. Custom House). It became one of the largest and best run retail brokerage firms in the country. In 1987, it relocated to midtown to even larger quarters just prior to being absorbed by Shearson Lehman Brothers.

(Right) Behind the tree is the Cunard Line Building at 25 Broadway, completed in 1921 and designed by Benjamin Morris. It is presently the headquarters of Standard & Poor's Corporation.

The House of Morgan

There are no twinkling lights on this Christmas wreath at 23 Wall Street, for that is not Morgan's style. Also in keeping with their understated approach is the total absence of any plaque or name plate. Customers simply know that this is where the Morgan firm has been located for almost a century.

The intersection of Wall and Broad Streets—the very center of the financial community—is not dominated by any tall buildings, yet each is imposing in its own way.

When J.P. Morgan purchased the site at 23 Wall Street, perhaps the most highly coveted in the Wall Street area, it was assumed that he would follow the tradition of others and build a tall, massive structure to justify the price he paid. But Morgan, true to his own ways, commissioned only a four-story building, with the upper two recessed so as to be invisible from the street. After all, this was not the place where those with bank accounts were keeping their household funds on deposit. The resulting design was understated, a little austere, and an act of conspicuous consumption on the grandest scale. There were private offices and dining rooms on the upper floors, topped by a small roof garden. There was no towering office building with rental income to provide maintenance, no restaurant in the basement— only a large banking hall with a few offices on one of the most highly regarded pieces of property in New York's highest rent district.

Morgan took up residence across the street on the 31st floor of the Bankers Trust Company Building, in the famous pyramid, in order to watch the construction of his new bank building. Unfortunately, he died in 1913, the year before its completion. On September 16, 1920, a wagonload of explosives, presumably set off by an anarchist interested in the demise of J.P. Morgan, Jr., exploded near 23 Wall Street. The deep pock marks visible today are reminders of this tragic episode.

19

J.P. Morgan & Co.

This is the famous banking room at J.P. Morgan & Co., 23 Wall Street. The chandelier consists of over nineteen hundred crystal pieces—known as pendeloques, oysters, balloons, and plugs—many of which were cut in Austria in the late nineteenth century. The largest one is a faceted crystal orb ten inches in diameter and weighing thirty-five pounds. The entire chandelier weighs approximately the equivalent of a Packard.

J. Pierpont Morgan established J.P. Morgan & Co. in New York in 1860 as the correspondent of J.S. Morgan & Co., a London merchant bank whose managing partner was his father. His principal business was dealing as agent in bills of exchange. The old Philadelphia investment banking firm of Drexel & Co. joined Morgan in 1871. (When J.P. Morgan & Co. was incorporated in 1940, its ties with Drexel & Co. were severed).

Innovative financings have become routine at J.P. Morgan & Co. over the years. The firm was instrumental in organizing General Electric Company, United States Steel Corporation, and International Harvester Corporation. It was a leading syndicator of securities for American Telephone & Telegraph Corporation as well as other domestic and foreign companies and governments. As early as 1838 its predecessor was arranging a loan in London for the State of Maryland, which had just gone into bankruptcy. And its prospectus for a French government issue in 1870 was transmitted in both English and French from London to Paris with a fleet of carrier pigeons carrying tissue paper pages rolled into capsules.

In 1909 President Taft asked J.P. Morgan to head a group of banks to assist China in the construction of an overland railway. In the United States it played a leading role in the reorganization of most of the major railroads, issuing 100-year bonds in many cases.

The Banking Act of 1933 required the firm to divest itself of its underwriting business. Several partners left to form Morgan Stanley & Co. in 1935. J.P. Morgan & Co. became a corporation in 1940 and in that year set up a trust operation which prior thereto it had been denied due to its partnership status. It raised additional capital stock through an offering managed by Smith Barney & Co. and set about building its investment department. At first it had approximately $300 million of advisory business, primarily the pension fund of Carnegie Corporation and endowments of the Phillips Exeter Academy, St. Paul's School, and Amherst College. Trust accounts soon arrived from George Whitney and others, followed by the extensive estate of J.P. Morgan in 1942. In 1959 the firm merged with Guaranty Trust Company, an old New York institution that had been founded in 1864, just four years after J.P. Morgan & Co.

The world of finance has been changing, especially in the last decade. As J.P. Morgan's traditional clients (primarily international corporations, institutions, and governments) have turned more to the securities markets to raise funds and have sought corporate finance advice on acquisitions, the firm has initiated new services, including underwriting and market making. It has become a leading Eurobond underwriter in London. Now its New York unit, J. P. Morgan Securities Inc., has been permitted by the Federal Reserve Governors to deal in debt securities. Its July 13, 1989 offering of 9.20% notes for the Xerox Corporation marked the first such activity by a commercial bank affiliate in the United States since the Glass-Steagall Act.

The Bank of New York at 48 Wall Street

Established by Alexander Hamilton in 1784, this is New York's oldest bank and one of only a handful of U.S. corporations that have existed for over 200 years. The bank was organized at the end of the Revolutionary War, when the population of New York had been depleted by half and the Continental currencies were worthless. The bank was capitalized with specie, precious metal coinage of foreign governments (Bavaria, Venice, France, and Spain, for example). There was no federal coinage until 1792. In New York the unit of exchange was the Spanish silver dollar. Thus, the need to establish a bank, to accept deposits and issue notes, was apparent.

Banks were not universally favored, however. In fact, many viewed them as inherently evil because they banished gold and silver and substituted paper. Their fees were questioned, as was the interference with the rapport between known creditors and debtors. However, the Bank of New York continued to sail its course and gradually proved the need for a central credit institution to enable the city's economy not only to recover to pre-war levels but expand beyond.

In 1797 the Bank of New York moved to a new two-story Georgian building at the corner of Wall and William Streets. It has been located here ever since, except for a brief period in 1799 when it moved to Greenwich Village after an outbreak of yellow fever that took 10 percent of the city's population.

A new building for the Bank was built in 1857-58 at 48

Wall, designed by Calvert Vaux, an English architect who collaborated with Frederick Law Olmstead in the design of Central Park. The building was expanded through the addition of two upper floors in 1879. This permitted an innovation—a luncheon room for officers and clerks. Until well into the twentieth century precise rules of conduct were observed. Each employee ate at a prescribed time and sat at an assigned seat under the watchful eyes of supervisors; female employees sat at separate tables. But the savings to the staff through lunches purchased on the premises, and the savings of time otherwise lost by workers going out, convinced the bank that this was a wise program.

The Bank of New York merged with the New York Life Insurance and Trust Company (established in 1830) in 1922; with the Fifth Avenue Bank in 1948; the Empire Trust Company in 1966; the County Trust Company in 1967; and with Irving Trust Company in 1989. Today the Bank's parent, the Bank of New York Company, Inc., ranks as the tenth largest bank holding company in the United States.

The magnificent Renaissance Revival building at 48 Wall Street shown in these photographs was designed by Benjamin Morris and completed in 1928. Morris also designed the Cunard Line Building at 25 Broadway and the Seamen's Bank for Savings (now owned by the American Insurance Group) at 72 Wall Street.

The Bank of New York at One Wall Street

This extraordinary Art Deco-inspired interior belongs to the Irving Trust Company, which merged with Bank of New York in 1989. The Irving headquarters, previously located in the Woolworth Building (a major client), moved to One Wall Street in 1932. Its building, including a lofty fifty-story limestone tower, was designed by Voorhees, Gmelin & Walker.

The main banking hall is believed to be the only room in the world entirely covered with mosaic tiles. Its ceiling is 37 feet high, and the interior was adapted from the *Stadshuser* (city hall) in Stockholm. The mosaic tiles are gold, orange, and red. They were manufactured in Berlin and account for approximately 9,000 square feet. This is the largest installation of mosaics in modern times.

On the 49th floor the bank built its equally unique board of directors' room and observatory. The ceiling is covered with iridescent kappa shells from the Philippines.

The Irving Trust Company was founded in 1851. Since

there was not yet a federal currency, each bank issued its own paper, and those institutions with the most appealing names found their certificates more widely accepted. Some banks, such as the Bank of the Metropolis, tried the imposing image. Irving selected another route and named the bank after Washington Irving, an author, diplomat, and lawyer who had gained an international reputation as America's first man of letters. His portrait appeared on the bank's notes and contributed to their wide appeal.

By the turn of the century Irving began to acquire nine of the city's many banking institutions, such as the New York Exchange Bank in 1912 and the Mercantile National Bank in 1913. Also in that year it relocated to new quarters in the Woolworth Building, which it occupied until moving to One Wall Street in 1931. Only two other structures are known to have occupied the site at Wall Street and Broadway, one of which by coincidence housed the law offices of Washington Irving.

Citibank's Downtown Headquarters

The great trading room of the Merchant's Exchange is one of Wall Street's grandest interiors. The Exchange was designed by Isaiah Rogers and completed in 1842. It has a fireproof insulated floor (adapted from English mills) and represents a unique blend of monumental scale, simple design, and practical engineering. From 1863 to 1899 this was the United States Custom House and after that the headquarters of the First National Bank, which was founded in 1865. The National City Bank, which became known in 1929 as the City Bank Farmers Trust Company, was located at 20 Exchange Place. When First National Bank merged with the latter in 1955, they simply joined their offices with an overhead bridge across the street. The new bank was called the First National City Bank of New York, now also known officially simply as Citibank. It is the largest bank in the country and certainly one of the largest in the world.

Brown Brothers Harriman & Co.

The painting in the partners' room shows four brothers, George, John, William, and James, circa 1860. The statue in the entrance rotunda is of Alexander Brown, father of the four.

The firm traces its origins to December 1800, when Alexander Brown emigrated from Ireland and established an "Irish Linen Warehouse" in Baltimore. Additional produce besides linen, as well as foreign exchange, was added to the activities of the firm, which his sons joined—first William, then George, John, and James. John A. Brown & Co. was established by the third son in Philadelphia in 1818 and it is from this firm that the present-day Brown Brothers Harriman & Co. descends. By the early 1820s, Alex Brown had become one of America's first millionaires. Brown Brothers opened its first office in New York in 1825 and rapidly became one of the principal merchant banking firms supplying credit and foreign exchange to New York's growing market.

The firm grew to specialize in guaranteed bills of exchange, which enabled exporters of merchandise to receive payment on a timely basis. The Brown family also maintained a direct interest in transportation, owning several sailing ships and steamers and even helping to establish the Baltimore & Ohio Railroad.

On May 1, 1929, they moved into a new skyscraper at 59 Wall Street, designed by Delano & Aldrich. Brown Brothers & Co. merged with Harriman Brothers & Co. in January 1931. In 1933, the firm elected to stay in the area of commercial banking, and the partners who preferred investment banking left to form a new company, initially called Brown Harriman & Co. in 1934 and then Harriman Ripley & Co. in 1938. Averell Harriman remained a partner of Brown Brothers Harriman & Co. while his ownership of Harriman Ripley was placed in a trust. Brown Brothers Harriman & Co. left the investment banking business on June 16, 1934, concentrating instead on private commercial banking. Over the years, it has remained a unique institution on Wall Street. It is a securities broker and member of the New York and other principal exchanges. It is also a wholesale commercial bank, taking deposits and making loans. And it is an investment manager and corporate finance specialist operating on a global basis.

The U.S. Trust Corporation

Organized in 1853, this is the oldest trust company in the country. Abraham Lincoln personally signed its charter. The founder was a young actuary with the United States Life Insurance Company in New York, John Stewart, whose idea was to start a company to act as executor and trustee for the funds of individuals and corporations. By June 10, 1853, the Trust Company had organized a board of trustees of thirty prominent New York merchants, bankers, industrialists, and civic leaders (including the mayor of New York). The offices were in rented space at 40 Wall Street—the Bank of Manhattan Company.

In those days the variety of investments was limited at best. Fixed-income securities were available only from the federal government, three states, and three railroads. On the New York Stock Exchange shares of just twenty-four companies were traded in 1853: eleven railroads, three banks, three insurance companies, three coal companies, two mining companies, one canal company, and two other enterprises.

The first corporate trust account came in 1855, when the United States Trust Company of New York was named registrar for the New York Central Railroad. But banking business—commercial and personal loans, plus mortgages—continued to be the mainstay of the Trust Company's operations. In 1868, prompted by an increase in its business, U.S. Trust moved from its location at 40 Wall Street to the Atlantic Mutual Insurance Co. Building at the corner of Wall and William Streets. Also in 1868 the trans-

continental railway link was completed, opening up the West Coast to the commerce and industry of the East. U.S. Trust participated in this growth, but then there were setbacks—financial panics in 1874 and again in 1884. The Trust Company's conservative management enabled it to ride out the storms, and by 1886 it led all other New York banks in deposit rankings with a total of just over $30 million.

U.S. Trust has occupied the site at 45 Wall Street for almost 125 years, a remarkable accomplishment for any organization, few of which have survived such a long time, let alone still be in the same location. Additional offices have been opened, in 1979 on Fifty-fourth Street next door to the University Club, in 1981 at 770 Broadway —the old Wanamaker Building—and in Palm Beach, Los Angeles, and Dallas in 1982, 1986, and 1989, respectively. Its headquarters were relocated to a newly constructed building on Forty-seventh Street in 1989.

Today U.S. Trust provides a wide variety of trust, investment, and banking services to clients throughout the country and the world. It also is a leader in the development of computer systems to deliver its services efficiently. Clients include individuals, corporations, institutions, governments, and fiduciaries. It is one of the largest managers of personal wealth in the country, and it is the nation's largest fiduciary.

Bankers Trust Company

(Above) Reflected in a glass table top is the pyramid atop the Bankers Trust Company Building at 14-16 Wall Street and the bold classic superstructure of the Equitable Building. They form Wall Street's own Acropolis.

Bankers Trust Company commissioned its new building in 1912 from Trowbridge & Livingston, who also designed 23 Wall Street for J.P. Morgan. In fact the pyramid —the Bankers Trust logo—was Morgan's downtown resi-

dence, where he stayed to keep an eye on his own building going up across the street. When it was completed, the Bankers Trust Building was considered the world's tallest structure on a small plot. For many years it has remained the most distinctive peak in the Wall Street range.

This company was founded in 1903 as a trust company for the existing commercial banks, which were precluded from engaging in trust business at the time. Therefore, in fact as well as in name, it was a trust company for banks. The banks were not allowed to perform any fiduciary services, and it is for this principal reason that J.P. Morgan and other colleagues were instrumental in the forming of Bankers Trust Company.

With the passage of the Federal Reserve Act of 1914, which granted trust privileges to national banks for the first time, Bankers Trust decided, for competitive reasons, that it should enter commercial banking on a full scale. It acquired the Astor Trust Co. in 1917 and, in 1922, was one of the first American banks to open an office in London. Its trust activities flourished during the 1930s as the bank was called upon to act as trustee in the safekeeping of collateral and in reorganizations.

World War II brought many changes in the way Americans lived and did business. The bond campaigns made investors of many people who never before had owned securities of any kind. Checks were being used by many people whose only banking contact in past years had been a savings account.

As a result, Bankers Trust—founded as an institution that accepted reserve deposits only and, according to leg-

end, once had asked a corporate customer to remove its account because it had drawn three checks in a month against its $1 million balance—had completed a 180-degree turn.

The bank expanded its operations in the state as well as worldwide. It saw the need of additional capital and offered $100 million of 25-year 4½% capital notes in 1963, the first issue of its kind by a major bank. With the annual volume of customer checks reaching 120 million by 1962 and growing at the rate of 65,000 a day, the bank pioneered in check processing systems and was the first in New York to provide checks with magnetic ink code numbers.

New facilities were built at 280 Park Avenue in 1962 and at One Bankers Trust Plaza, 130 Liberty Street, in 1974. Expansion continued overseas with the opening of offices in 35 countries. Its non-banking activities have reached the point where Bankers Trust is a major participant in private placements, mergers and acquisitions, currency transactions, and securities underwriting. With the exception of underwriting corporate equity obligations, it is by all accounts a large and eminently successful investment bank. Bankers Trust sold nearly all of its retail branches in 1979 and 1980, concentrating more on wholesale banking and trust activities.

The success of the bank's redirected focus on merchant and wholesale banking is demonstrated in its strong earnings performance (an increase of 568 percent during the ten years ended 1988) and its high degree of profitability —one of the most profitable major banks in the country.

Sixty and Forty Wall Street

(Opposite) J.P. Morgan & Co.'s new office tower at 60 Wall Street was completed in 1989, designed by Kevin Roche, John Dinkeloo & Associates. This fifty-five-story building replicates, in contemporary terms, the elements of a classical column (base shaft and capital). Its height was made possible through the transfer of air-rights from 55 Wall Street.

(Above) Forty Wall Street was built in 1929 by Craig Severance and Yasuo Matsui as the headquarters of the Bank of the Manhattan Company, which had originally been organized in 1799 at this same location.

For many years some of Wall Street's greatest firms have been located at 40 Wall Street, including Loeb, Rhodes & Co. and Bache & Co., each with their private entrances, and Kuhn, Loeb & Co. and White, Weld & Co. In more recent years, foreign affiliates such as Deutsche Bank Capital Corporation and The Toronto-Dominion Bank have been headquartered here. The firm with one of the longest tenures to date is Winthrop, Stimson, Putnam & Roberts, which has been headquartered here for almost forty years.

The Chase Manhattan Bank

(Opposite) All dressed up with their Christmas lights, Chase Manhattan's trees dance across the plaza on their night off. A submerged garden of fountains and pools by Isamu Noguchi is sunk in the courtyard, surrounded by the ground-floor banking department. *(Above)* Outside the bank's plaza level is Jean Dubuffet's sculpture "Group of Four Trees" commissioned by David Rockefeller in 1972—a delightful forest of papier-mache trees providing a soft touch to the more serious steel walls of the Chase Manhattan Building. In the background is 40 Wall Street, headquarters to Bank of the Manhattan Company for many years.

The Manhattan Company was chartered in 1799 as a water company designed to bring fresh water into the city and curtail further outbreaks of yellow fever. One of its founders, Aaron Burr, persuaded the New York State legislature to allow the company to expand its activities into banking. On September 1, 1799, the Bank of the Manhattan Company opened an "office of discount and deposit" at 40 Wall Street. It entered into financing ship construction in 1805 and, among other projects, helped to finance the Erie Canal. In 1877, John Thompson, a financier and foreign currency specialist, founded Chase National Bank and named it for Salmon P. Chase, Secretary of the Treasury under Abraham Lincoln. Chase is considered the father of the modern banking system; he drafted the National Currency Act of 1863, which established a national currency and the present Federal banking system. His

portrait appears on the largest bill in circulation ($10,000).

The Bank of the Manhattan Company developed the first machine for sorting checks in 1935. In 1955 it merged with Chase National (which had become the largest bank in the world in 1930), forming the Chase Manhattan Bank. In 1959, Chase opened one of the first corporate computer facilities and became the first to have a fully automated check processing system.

Automation has expanded to the point where Chase is the world leader in domestic and international money transfers. It is also one of the two largest bank issuers of credit cards.

The Chase Manhattan Building was designed by Gordon Bunshaft of Skidmore, Owings & Merrill and completed in 1961. Bunshaft is best known for Lever House on Park Avenue, which instituted a whole new era of skyscrapers designed with open plazas for pedestrian circulation. The Chase building took five years to construct and sits on what was then the most expensive piece of real estate in the world. The building is the first major example of the International Style built downtown, the first to offer an open plaza where none had previously existed, the first to use the term "One Chase Manhattan Plaza," and the first to provide an anchor in an area where many firms were moving uptown. Several of Wall Street's most prestigious firms relocated here: Davis Polk & Wardwell; Milbank, Tweed, Hadley & McCloy; and Eastman Dillon, Union Securities & Co.

The Federal Reserve Bank of New York

Headquartered at 33 Liberty Street, this is the most important of twelve Federal Reserve Banks throughout the country. Completed in 1924, the structure was designed by York & Sawyer to resemble a fifteenth-century Florentine palace such as were built for only the wealthiest merchants. The architects here have used oversized limestone blocks to emphasize the fact that this is a banker's bank. It contains more gold than Fort Knox. In fact, the gold reserves of approximately eighty foreign nations are stored in its vaults, five levels below the street, possibly the largest accumulation of gold in the world. It moves from one account to another, almost never leaving the building.

Christmas at the New York Stock Exchange

The main building at Broad and Wall Streets was completed in 1903 and the 23-story tower building at Eleven Wall Street was completed in 1922.

The New York Stock & Exchange Board (the "NYS & EB") was formally organized on March 8, 1817 as a successor to the trading practices that had commenced in New York in 1792 under a buttonwood tree on lower Wall Street.

Members voted for candidates by placing a black or white ball in a box, and a fixed number of black balls constituted rejection for membership; the candidate was "black balled." Members were liable for fines of six to

twenty-five cents for absence, for not wearing their hats, and for interrupting the president as he "called" or read the names of each stock or bond twice each day. The members sat in their seats and bid for securities offered for sale. Hence a membership was referred to as a "seat."

In 1842 the NYS & EB moved to the new Merchants' Exchange at 55 Wall Street. By 1865 it had outgrown these facilities, owing in part to the increase of trading and speculating in securities during the Civil War. It officially changed its name to the New York Stock Exchange in 1863 and moved to a new building at 10-12 Broad Street (part of its present site) in 1865.

Broad and Wall Streets

(Opposite) Limousines (for hire) wait outside the New York Stock Exchange, whose main building (1903) was designed by George Post. It duplicates the Greek Revival temple design of the Federal Hall National Memorial across the street with its own columned facade, adding a frieze of life-size figures in its pediment. The 23-story tower was designed by Trowbridge & Livingston (who also did J.P. Morgan & Co.) and completed in 1922. Additional trading space known as the "garage" was located on the street level of this building.

(Above) The statue of George Washington in front of the Federal Hall National Memorial. It is at the location shown here that Washington was sworn in as the nation's first president in 1789. New York City was then the capitol, and, although the war had ended six years earlier, the nation still had some disagreements among the states.

Just to the right is the Seamen's Bank for Savings at 30 Wall Street, also home for many years to Kuhn, Loeb & Co. This building was designed by York & Sawyer in 1919 as the United States Assay Office. Seamen's Bank, which was organized in 1829 as one of the first savings banks in the country, moved here in 1955.

Federal Hall National Memorial

Located at 26 Wall Street, this is the finest example of a Greek Revival temple in New York. The design by Ithiel Town and Alexander Davis is inspired by the Parthenon, but the original dome was modified into a rotunda with a deep entablature and a two-story colonnade.

The building was completed in 1842, replacing the original Federal Hall where George Washington was sworn in as the country's first president in 1789. It served as the nation's Custom House until 1862 and then as the United States Subtreasury until 1920. It has been a Federal monument since then.

Wall Street, South Street

Many a rapid fortune has been made in this street, and many a no less rapid ruin. Some of these very merchants whom you see hanging about here now have locked up money in their strong-boxes, like the man in the Arabian Nights, and, opening them again, have found but withered leaves. Below, here by the water-side, where the bowsprits of ships stretch across the footway, and almost thrust themselves into the windows, lie the noble American vessels which have made their packet service the finest in the world.

They have brought hither the foreigners who abound in all the streets: not, perhaps, that there are more here than in other commercial cities; but elsewhere they have particular haunts, and you must find them out; here they pervade the town.

Charles Dickens
American Notes, 1842

One Wall Street

This has been headquarters of the Irving Trust Company prior to its 1989 acquisition by the Bank of New York. This Art Deco structure was built in 1932 and designed by Voorhees, Gmelin & Walker. On the side of the entrance to One Wall Street is a plaque commemorating the history of the street. In 1653 a wall of planks and rails was erected to protect Nieu Amsterdam from invasion by both Indians and the British. It extended across the island to Pearl Street and was called *de Waal*. The attack did not come until eleven years later, by sea, and the wall never served its purpose. The British tore it down in 1699.

Lee Higginson & Co.

The Greek temple at 37 Broad Street was built in 1932, designed by Cross & Cross as the headquarters of Lee Higginson & Co., one of the greatest names in investment banking during the first quarter of this century.

While many firms survived the stock market collapse of 1929, Ivar Kreugar, the "Swedish Match King," dealt a near-fatal blow to venerable Lee Higginson and a handful of other firms, including J.P. Morgan, duping them out of over a quarter of a billion dollars and then committing suicide in his Paris apartment in March of 1932. Lee Higg, as it was known, eventually disappeared into Hayden Stone in 1966. Its building was long ago taken over by Bank of America's International operations who have now, in turn, let this magnificent temple be occupied by a dress shop.

Fraunces Tavern

This tavern at 54 Pearl Street is largely a reconstruction of the original Georgian-style residence and tavern. Its reconstruction, completed in 1907 by William Mersereau, was based on a house originally built in 1719 as a residence for Etienne de Lancey, who sold it in 1762 to Samuel Fraunces, an innkeeper. The New York State Chamber of Commerce was founded here in 1768 during a meeting called to protest British trade policies. And six years later American patriots met here to plan New York's version of the Boston Tea Party. George Washington made his farewell address to his troops here on December 4, 1783. Six years later and a few blocks away he was inaugurated as first president of the United States, at Federal Hall. Samuel Fraunces was there as his steward.

This site was the entrance to Nieu Amsterdam. Pearl Street ringed the edge of the city and Broad Street was originally a canal extending up to where the Dow Jones Building was, just short of Exchange Place. In 1614, Captain Adriaen Block launched the *Onrust* at this intersection, the first ship built on Manhattan. His previous ship had burned the year before, forcing him and his crew to construct what were to be the first Dutch dwellings here and spend the winter. Captain Block returned to the Netherlands in 1614, sailing up the coast of America and discovering Block Island, for whom he is best remembered, on his way home.

Coenties Slip and Pearl Street

Pearl Street is named for the oyster shells that once lined the shores of the city and were used to pave this street. Its neighbor, Stone Street, was the first to be paved with cobblestones. Coenties Slip was named for a Dutch family who once lived here. The slip was filled in around 1835.

The first City Hall originally stood at this intersection on Pearl Street. It was built in 1642 originally as an inn for the many traders and settlers who were crowding into the city. In 1653 Peter Stuyvesant turned the inn into the *Stadt Huys*. In the photograph are nineteenth-century warehouses of the Fraunces Tavern Block Historic District, built primarily from 1829 to 1858 on the city's first landfill, which dates back to 1689.

The expansion of new buildings in the Wall Street area was enhanced by the demolition of the Pearl Street Elevated in 1950-51. Fifty-five Water Street was built in 1971 by Emery Roth & Sons—the largest privately financed office building in the world at the time.

The Coenties Slip buildings were threatened by a plan for a parking lot but were granted national landmark status in 1977 (and local status the following year). They are now referred to as the Fraunces Tavern Block Historic District.

One of the casualties, however, was the old Seamen's Church Institute Building (1909-1969) which resembled more of a downtown "Y" than anything else. But its vast cafeteria steam tables provided affordable lunches. During my first summer at Glore, Forgan & Co., I had colleagues in similar underpaid management apprenticeships at Kuhn Loeb; F.I. du Pont; and Goodbody. We would meet regularly at the Seamen's Institute for cheap lunches; we always referred to it as "the Yacht Club."

When Goldman Sachs began construction of its new facilities at 85 Broad Street, it unearthed remains of seventeenth-century dwellings, which are now carefully preserved in glass-topped sidewalk displays.

Goldman, Sachs & Co.

The headquarters building of this firm at 85 Broad Street, designed by Skidmore, Owings & Merrill, was completed in 1983. Its lobby curves to conform to the shape of Stone Street over which it was built. Originally this site was purchased by Lehman Brothers, who were going to build their own new headquarters to replace the cramped One William Street offices. But the economic downturn of 1973-75 changed all that, and now Goldman Sachs, its friendly competitor for many years, occupies the spot instead.

In 1882 Marcus Goldman and Samuel Sachs formed a partnership to continue a commercial paper business which had been started by Goldman in 1869. It has operated under the name Goldman, Sachs & Co. since 1885 and remains the only major partnership on Wall Street today.

From the early days when Marcus Goldman would walk the streets of Manhattan negotiating trade receivables among merchants and banks, stuffing the receipts in the lining of his top hat, the firm has maintained a unique, close-knit entrepreneurial spirit. When asked some years ago if Goldman Sachs had a new business department, Walter Sachs replied that "Goldman Sachs & Co. *is* a new business department."

The firm joined the New York Stock Exchange in 1896 and entered the field of investment banking in 1906, when it co-managed its first public offering for United Cigars Manufacturers which is still one of the firm's clients. Goldman Sachs was a pioneer in underwriting public offerings and brought many issues to market for well-known names in retailing and consumer goods manufacturing. In the 1930s, the firm began making markets in securities, and it developed institutional and individual sales departments.

In 1956, Goldman Sachs was co-manager of the first public offering of Ford Motor Company common stock, the largest equity offering ever undertaken and a major event in corporate finance history. The syndicate contained an unprecedented number of underwriters—*seven hundred twenty-two*—clearly the greatest assemblage of firms ever. Partners of firms competing to manage the offering all began driving Fords that year. At Goldman Sachs some still do or, as the above photograph shows, Lincolns and Mercurys.

Today Goldman Sachs is a leading, full-service investment banking and securities firm with 132 general and 55 limited partners and approximately 6300 employees. It has occupied various Broad Street sites, primarily nos. 20, 55, and 85, for over thirty years.

The Stone and Webster Building

For many years this building at 90 Broad Street, designed by Cross & Cross in 1930, was the Stone & Webster Building, New York headquarters to the engineering firm founded in 1889. It was also headquarters to Stone & Webster Securities Corporation which was organized in 1927. This firm was involved in so many engineering and construction projects for its clients that it decided to help underwrite securities to finance them. In fact, the tremendous growth of the natural gas pipelines in the 1950s—primarily Tennessee Gas Transmission Corp. (Tenneco) and Trans-continental Gas Pipeline Corp. (Transco), whose securities the firm underwrote with White, Weld & Co.—helped secure Stone & Webster a solid place in the lineup of major bracket firms. It conducted a full range of investment banking and brokerage services and, together with White Weld, pioneered in innovative financings for clients that had large appetites for capital funds, creating the use of debt with warrants, convertibles, and other similar instruments. In 1974 Stone & Webster decided to terminate its securities affiliate.

The Standard Oil Company Building

The famous Standard Oil Company Building at 26 Broadway was completed in 1922 and designed by Carrère & Hastings, who also designed the New York Public Library and the home of Henry Frick (now the Frick Collection). This address was home for many years to the Standard Oil Company of New York (SOCONY), which was later called Socony-Vacuum, then Socony-Mobil, and now Mobil Corp. In 1956 the company moved uptown. Around the top of the lobby frieze are carved the names of the original directors of the company. The Christmas tree in the photograph is a special one, with large, old-fashioned lights and silver tinsel, straight out of the 1940s.

Steamship Row Lobbies

(Above) The facilities at the Cunard Line Building, 25 Broadway, are now occupied by Standard & Poor's Corporation, and those at One Broadway by Citibank. This area was once known as "Steamship Row" from the large number of steamship companies maintaining their offices here. Even today, clients of Citibank may elect to enter through either the First Class or Cabin Class entrances. The Tourist Class entrance sign has been removed. Once inside, however, the service is all First Class.

(Opposite) One Broadway was home for many years to the United States Lines, best known for its flagship of the same name. On her maiden voyage in 1952, the *S.S. United States* established a world's record for crossing time between New York and Southhampton: three days and eighteen hours, which still stands today, almost forty years later. Her secret was classified until recently, and then the government decided to let us in on the deal: she had four engines. She also was the only ship built with duplicate machinery, wiring and fittings in case of any mechanical failure.

Cunard Line Building

The main attraction of the Cunard Line Building is its booking hall. The dome is sixty-five feet high and the entire space is covered with murals by Ezra Winter and maps by Barry Faulkner. It was a fitting statement for the most prestigious steamship company of a nation that claimed to rule the seas.

Cunard was one of the greatest transportation companies in the world when this building, designed by Benjamin Morris, opened in 1921. Cunard was founded in 1840 and merged with the White Star Line (1871) in 1934. The names of Cunard's ships always ended in "*ia*" such as *Lusitania, Mauretania,* and *Aquitania*. The White Star ships ended in "*ic*" such as *Olympic, Britannic,* and *Titanic*. In 1934, the chairman of Cunard Line, Sir Peter Bates, informed King George that the largest steamship company in the world would build the largest passenger ship and name it for England's greatest queen. King George acknowledged the disclosure and said he was pleased that it would be named for his wife. And thus, in an interesting turn of events, the new ship was christened the *Queen Mary* and not the *Queen Victoria* as Cunard Line had planned, in keeping with its *-ia* nomenclature tradition.

In 1977 the United States Postal Service moved its Bowling Green Station to this location from the Custom House.

The United States Custom House

This distinguished palace is a monumental statement to New York's role as a great seaport. It was designed by Cass Gilbert and completed in 1907. Gilbert also designed the Woolworth Building. If the latter, with its elaborate Gothic interior and mosaic icons, is referred to as the "Cathedral of Commerce," then the U.S. Custom House is certainly the "Temple of Commerce."

Because of the preeminence of the port of New York, this was the largest custom house in the country, and, prior to the creation of a federal income tax in 1913, it was the largest collector of funds for the government. Therefore, its grand structure seems fitting. Together with Grand Central Terminal, it is one of the greatest Beaux Arts buildings in New York. It was built using the latest technology but is wrapped in the exuberant decoration and expansive forms characteristic of the 1860s and 1870s—a rich display to convey the image of power and wealth and called Beaux Arts style after the Ecole des Beaux-Arts in Paris.

For many years the Customs Service was located in the

Merchants' Exchange building at 55 Wall Street. But it had outgrown its space at the turn of the century, a time when the United States had become a significant world power with a strong navy and manufacturing capacity. The government therefore wanted a structure that would reflect its new standing.

The building is basically a modern steel skeleton clad in the fashionable Beaux Arts style. The rotunda employs a new vaulting system and contains an elliptical 140-ton skylight matching the shape of the large counter below.

The rotunda is covered with a flat timbrel vault whose technical design traces its origins to Byzantium, that was imported to the United States in 1881. The system uses thin clay tiles laid in several layers bound by mortar. The eggshell-thin laminated structure is sturdy, light, and fireproof. A traditional vault relies on friction, gravity and lateral thrust for support—more expensive and time-consuming to construct. Timbrel vaults have also been used at the Cathedral of St. John the Divine and St. Thomas' Church on Fifth Avenue.

Bowling Green

The site of the Custom House *(opposite)* is Fort Amsterdam, the original defense center of the Dutch colony. It was built from 1638 to 1646 and renamed Fort James when the British claimed Nieu Amsterdam in 1664. King Charles II wanted to unite his colonies in New England and the Mid-Atlantic by taking New Netherland. Peter Stuyvesant was unable to muster the barest semblance of a fighting force and surrendered without a single shot being fired. The new city was named in honor of King Charles' brother James, Duke of York. But in 1673, the Dutch forces marched back into the city and reclaimed it, calling it New Orange; the fort was called Fort Willem Hendrick. The

following year the Dutch withdrew and New Orange became New York, once and for all.

Customs business had been conducted at various locations near Bowling Green until the service moved to Federal Hall in 1842 and to the Merchants' Exchange Building in 1863. It was located at Bowling Green from 1907 to 1973, after which it relocated to the World Trade Center.

This structure by Cass Gilbert is an important anchor to the city's past, in an environment that seems to have no past. It has fifty-four massive Corinthian columns, a grand arched entrance, and four massive sculptures by Daniel Chester French.

In the foreground of the photograph is Bowling Green, the site where Peter Minuit negotiated the purchase of Manhattan for twenty-four dollars. He later built a residence where the United States Lines Building is today.

The green has been maintained as an open area since the earliest days. In fact, the fence around it was built in 1771-72 to protect a statue of King George and preserve the area. This fence is thus one of the oldest landmarks in lower Manhattan. During construction of a new subway line in 1914, the fence was removed to Central Park, where it was forgotten and actually lost. It was finally discovered and returned, a marvel of urban survival.

The United States Lines Building (*opposite*), One Broadway, was originally built as the Washington Building by Edward Kendall in 1884. Just to the right is Eleven Broadway, built in 1893 as the headquarters for Spencer Trask & Co. He and J.P. Morgan were the original backers of Thomas Edison and were among the first subscribers to electric lights in 1882. Spencer Trask also had his own private branch wire system in 1881, thanks to Edison, and in the area of research, the firm established the first statistical securities department in 1894. Its director, John Moody, eventually branched out on his own with his Moody's Manual.

Snowstorm on Lower Broadway

(*Above*) The Cunard Line Building, 25 Broadway, designed by Benjamin Morris (1921) and *(opposite)* the Standard Oil Company Building, 26 Broadway, designed by Carrère & Hastings and Shreve, Lamb & Blake (1922).

These two neighbors, facing each other across Broadway, form a complementary balance. Both are quiet, dignified, and grand classical office buildings. The main attraction of the Cunard Line Building is its booking hall where, under ornate groin and domical vaults, people booked passage on the *Mauretania*, the *Queens* and other ships.

The Standard Oil Company Building is one of New York's great unappreciated structures. The base of the building follows the gentle curve of Bowling Green Park. The 480-foot high pyramidal tower, however, is set at an angle, aligning with the uptown grid of streets. Thus the building relates to two separate elements—the street level and the skyline. The total composition never appears disjointed. It is an interesting blend of two different environments in one building design.

Blessed are the Meek

(Above) A Wall Streeter takes time out during her lunch hour to tend to her flock in Battery Park. A light snow is falling around them.

> *Blessed are the poor in spirit,*
>   *for theirs is the kingdom of heaven.*
> *Blessed are those who mourn,*
>   *for they will be comforted.*
> *Blessed are the meek,*
>   *for they will inherit the earth.*
> *Blessed are those who hunger and thirst for righteousness,*
>   *for they will be filled.*
> *Blessed are the merciful,*
>   *for they will be shown mercy.*
> *Blessed are the pure in heart,*
>   *for they will see God.*
> *Blessed are the peacemakers,*
>   *for they will be called sons of God.*
> *Blessed are those who are persecuted because of righteousness,*
>   *for theirs is the kingdom of heaven.*
>   *Matthew 5: 3-10*

The Immigrants

(Opposite) This bronze sculpture by Luis Sanguino was installed in Battery Park in 1973. Between 1855 and 1890 an estimated 7.8 million immigrants passed through the Immigrant Landing Depot—now Castle Clinton. The structure was originally a fort and later a concert hall. But as an immigrant station it was overcrowded and ill equipped, forcing the government to relocate to spacious new facilities on Ellis Island in 1892.

In the background of the photograph are three buildings built by Emery Roth & Sons: One Battery Park Plaza (1971), 17 State Street (1989) and One State Street behind it (1969).

Herman Melville was born in 1819 in a house where 17 State Street now stands. The old Seamen's Church Institute, which began in 1834 with a Gothic chapel on a barge to provide pastoral care to sailors away from home, moved here from Coenties Slip in 1969; it lasted less than twenty years at this site. Its previous location, where it had been since 1909, was destroyed to make room for 55 Water Street. This section is known as Battery Park or simply the Battery.

The Battery was the name given to a row of cannons along the waterfront, where State Street is today, from Bowling Green to Whitehall. During the War of 1812, on a pile of rocks offshore was erected West Battery which became known later as Castle Clinton. The landfill in later years connected West Battery to the shore and transformed the area into Battery Park.

The New York Vietnam Veterans Memorial

(Above) This memorial was designed by Peter Wormser and William Fellows and completed in 1985. The memorial is a translucent wall of glass blocks upon which the letters of New Yorkers who died in Vietnam have been engraved. In a letter to his mother simply signed "Howie," one soldier writes:

"I worry more about the war back home than I do about my own life over here. What good is the peace we accomplish here if we don't have peace in our own back yards?"

This park was originally named Jeannette Park after the luckless ship of the same name that was lost, together with her entire crew, on an Arctic expedition in 1881. The expedition was sponsored by James Gordon Bennett, Jr., of the *New York Herald*, who had named the ship after his daughter. A memorial service to the lost seamen was held here in 1884 when the park was created. It sits on the bed of Coenties Slip.

A Street Vendor on Broad Street

(Opposite) This unusually wide, curved street was actually a canal, called *de Herre Gracht* ("the Gentlemen's Canal"). It reached to today's Exchange Place, where a ferry to Long Island docked. The canal was filled in during the 1680s when the Dutch began to push the city limits further out. Pearl Street was initially at the edge. Later came Water, Front and South Streets—all built on landfill. The wide section of Beaver Street stretching from Broad Street to Bowling Green offers a clue to its history: it too was originally a canal, called *de Begijn Gracht.*

Seen in the photograph are, from the left: One New York Plaza, 90 Broad Street (the Stone & Webster Building) and 70 Broad Street.

Whitehall

(Opposite) Commuters trudge to the Staten Island ferry on their way home. This area is called Whitehall, the site of Governor Peter Stuyvesant's house, built in 1658, which the British renamed "Whitehall" in 1664 when they took control of Nieu Amsterdam. The city was renamed that year in honor of James, Duke of York, heir presumptive to the throne of his brother, King Charles II.
(Above) Hunger and snow can humble even the loftiest executives.

The Battery Maritime Building

Originally, this was called the Municipal Ferry Piers and it has remained in continuous operation since opening in 1909. Presently the Coast Guard operates ferry service to Governors Island from here. By the turn of the last century, at the peak of ferry service, there were seventeen lines operating between terminals in Manhattan and Brooklyn. Now the only one with regularly-scheduled passenger service is the Staten Island ferry, although new service from New Jersey and Brooklyn appears from time to time, especially during the summer months.

CROSSING BROOKLYN FERRY

Flood-tide below me! I watch you face to face;
Clouds of the west! sun there half an hour high! I see you also face to face.

Crowds of men and women attired in the usual costumes! how curious you are to me!
On the ferry-boats, the hundreds and hundreds that cross, returning home, are more
    curious to me than you suppose;
And you that shall cross from shore to shore years hence, are more to me, and more in my
    meditations, than you might suppose...
It avails not, neither time or place—distance avails not;
I am with you, you men and women of a generation, or ever so many generations hence;
I project myself—also I return—I am with you, and know how it is.

Just as you feel when you look on the river and sky, so I felt;
Just as any of you is one of a living crowd, I was one of a crowd;
Just as you are refresh'd by the gladness of the river and the bright flow, I was refresh'd;
Just as you stand and lean on the rail, yet hurry with the swift current, I stood, yet was
    hurried;
Just as you look on the numberless masts of ships, and the thick-stem'd pipes of steamboats,
    I look'd...

These, and all else, were to me the same as they are to you;
I project myself a moment to tell you—also I return.

Walt Whitman
Leaves of Grass, (1881)

Broadway near Exchange Place

(*Above*) A snowplow clears the Irving Bank's sidewalks.
(*Opposite*) Across the street is 71 Broadway, built in 1894 as
the Empire Building but known for many years as the
U.S. Steel Company Building. It was designed by Renwick,
Aspinwall & Tucker. Presently this is the home of the
New York Society of Securities Analysts.

At this point, Broadway begins to manifest its main characteristic, which continues up to Columbia Heights. It is
the highest ridge on Manhattan—a backbone from which

side streets often gently slope. Broadway was originally
called *de Heere Straat* by the Dutch—"the Gentlemen's
Street." The British renamed its lower section Great George
Street and the section by Trinity Church, Church Walk.
Sections further north had various names, including the
Boulevard or Boulevard Lafayette. It was not until Febru-
ary 14, 1899 that the entire 15.5-mile street was given a
single name.

Stone Street

(Above) This view of Stone Street is taken from Goldman Sachs' plaza. Stone Street was the first to be paved with cobblestones. Pearl Street came next, with oyster shells.

Nassau Street

(Opposite) The financial district has its own *altstadt* ("old city"), in this case Nassau Street, which is so busily commercial that it can only be photographed at dusk and preferably during a snow storm. Nassau Street is named for King William III of the House of Orange-Nassau (for whom Princeton University's Nassau Hall is also named).

Many of the buildings in this area are richly decorated structures dating from the 1870s and 1880s. The original Keuffel & Essen Building (1893) is at 127 Fulton Street and an elaborate Bennett Building, built by James Bennett of the *New York Herald* (1889), is at 99 Nassau Street (at the right in the photograph). It has a deeply three-dimensional cast iron front that has been painted in creams and pastels. The *New York Herald* was one of the first subscribers to electricity in 1882, along with the *Evening Telegram*, which was started by Bennett's son. The power came from a private Edison plant built to service only these newspapers.

Wall Street Snowstorm

(Left) Pearl Street and Gerardi's in the snow. This has been a familiar landmark since 1932, as seasoned as Sweet's, Sloppy Louie's, and Harry's. Other less fortunate institutions exist only in memory, such as Masoletti's, which, until its demise in 1975, took personal checks but no plastic, and Eberlin's, whose captains owned territories and guaranteed to have you in and out in under twelve minutes so that the next customers could be seated. A second cup of coffee might easily wind up on one's shoulder as a warning salvo not to linger.

(Above, left) The old City Midday Club at 23 South Wil-

liam Street. (William Street was not named for King William III but rather for Willem Beeckman who served as mayor of Nieu Amsterdam for nine terms.) For many years this famous Wall Street luncheon club was located in this old Tudor-style building. It relocated to the top floors of 140 Broadway in 1967 and this structure became a public restaurant.

(Above, right) The India House at One Hanover Square. This structure, originally the headquarters of the Hanover Bank, was designed by Richard Carman and built between 1851 and 1854. It resembles a Florentine palazzo in New York brownstone, a material more commonly associated with uptown residences but once typical downtown as well. Handsome Corinthian columns and a fine balustrade create a distinguished doorway entrance. In addition to its role as headquarters of the Hanover Bank, India House served as the New York Cotton Exchange until 1886 and then as the headquarters of W.R. Grace & Co.

Two familiar Wall Street institutions share this landmark—the India House Broad Street Club upstairs and Harry's downstairs.

The India House

This 135-year-old house has been a private luncheon club since 1914. It was founded by James A. Farrell and others who had maritime as opposed to banking and securities interests. Its very name derives from the wealth of excitement, challenge and often prosperity from long voyages to the Indies, East and West, and to India. Throughout its spacious, residential-like facilities, the visitor is constantly reminded of its heritage by nautical paintings, ship models and several large Buddhas.

The rare ship models, engravings and paintings donated by James Farrell and Willard Straight, as well as the decorations of paintings by the American Asiatic Institute, constitute one of the greatest collections of maritime art in the country.

In the main reading room *(above)* of the India House, members catch up with the latest shipping news in the *Journal of Commerce* under the watchful eyes of former directors (on the left) or Buddha himself (on the right).

On a Clear Day You Can See the Singer Building

Pause for a minute and reflect on this rare photo mural of New York in the 1940s. It was taken from a member's ship and is mounted on the walls of the India House bar room. The photograph could have been taken anytime between 1931 (the Cities Service Building) and 1960 (when Chase Manhattan Plaza was going up). The distinctive rounded profile of the Singer Building is approximately equidistant between the Woolworth and Irving Bank towers. Note the solid, classical motifs of many of these buildings, virtually all of which are there today but ringed with an outer layer of modern boxes.

The evolution of the financial district's architecture had been slow up until the 1960s. Along the waterfront were many three- and four-storied commercial structures, like those of Schermerhorn Row on Fulton Street. The larger buildings of the banks and brokerage houses were clustered around Wall and Broad Streets— the inland blocks. The solid dignity of this center was ringed by a collection of older buildings. As the *New York Times* architecture critic Paul Goldberger has said, the world of Louis Auchincloss and that of Horatio Alger kept each other in check.

With the need for expansion, all of this changed. The Chase Manhattan bank was the first major office building downtown since the 1930s. But the available land at the center was soon absorbed and the expansion moved to the water's edge: Fifty-Five Water Street, the New York Plaza collection, the Schroder Building, and the World Trade Center and World Financial Center. The area has its own skyline—a larger group of waterfront skyscrapers than anywhere else.

There was Babylon and Nineveh, they were built of brick. Athens was goldmarble columns. Rome was held up on broad arches of rubble. In Constantinople the minarets flame like great candles round the Golden Horn...

Steel, glass, tile, concrete will be the materials of the skyscrapers. Crammed on the narrow island the millionwindowed buildings will jut, glittering pyramid on pyramid, white cloudsheads piled above a thunderstorm.

John Dos Passos
Manhattan Transfer, (1925)

Upstairs at the India House

This is the main dining room of the India House; its Indian curried dishes are renowned. The main dining room can accommodate two hundred members and guests plus an additional two hundred thirty in the club's ten private rooms upstairs. Presently India House has approximately eleven hundred members from all sectors of the maritime and financial communities.

City Bank Farmers Trust Company

This is the executive dining room of the City Bank Farmers Trust Company at 20 Exchange Place. The Farmers Loan & Trust Company (1822) merged with the National City Bank (1812) in 1929. They moved into this magnificent fifty-seven story building in 1931. The unusual Art Deco lobby employs forty-five different marbles and a new combination of nickel and copper in its decorative motifs. The dining room shown here has its own fireplace and cherry wood paneling to remind its executives of an English manor house.

When the bank merged with the First National Bank, whose headquarters were at 55 Wall Street, they built a bridge across Exchange Place to join the two buildings. The street derives its name from the 55 Wall Street structure: the Merchants' Exchange.

Banca Commerciale Italiana

"BCI," as it is known abroad, is the second largest bank in Italy in terms of deposits. It was established in Milan in 1894 and immediately set the pace in Italy's economic and financial world. The bank's overseas network began before World War I and continued on an increasing scale in the 1950s with the opening of its own branches and the acquisition (together with other leading foreign banks) of shareholdings in local banks and finance institutions.

This is the largest of the three banks of National Interest (the others being Credito Italiano and Banco di Roma) controlled by IRI, the Istituto per la Ricostruzione Industriale, Rome, an Italian government entity. IRI pres-

ently owns 59 percent of the shares of BCI; the rest are in the hands of over 40,000 shareholders. The shares are listed on the Milan, Genoa, Rome and Turin stock exchanges.

As a short-term credit institution, BCI engages in all forms of commercial banking. In addition, it owns minority participations in a number of credit institutions active in medium and long-term banking, such as Mediobanca and Credito Fondiario. The bank is also active in leasing and factoring. It has been doing business in the United States since 1918.

J. & W. Seligman & Co. Incorporated

This investment firm was founded in 1864 by Joseph Seligman and his seven brothers. Originally the brothers ran a dry goods business. In New York, the Seligmans were located for a time at One William Street, on whose site they built the Seligman building in 1907. In its early years, the firm helped finance the U.S. Government's Civil War by placing $200 million of its bonds in Europe—an undertaking as difficult as stopping Lee at Gettysburg. The $500-denominated bonds were engraved with the statement that they bore interest at 10 cents per day. But the Europeans were not impressed with the credit. Later, J. & W. Seligman & Co. was appointed the U.S. Navy's Fiscal Agent by President Grant, joined the New York Stock Exchange in 1869 (and thus is one of its oldest members), and helped finance a broad spectrum of industrial America, from railroads to motor cars and talking machines. It also helped finance the Panama Canal and raised billions of dollars for Great Britain, France, and Italy during World War I. Today it is primarily an investment advisory firm, managing portfolios for pension funds, individual investors, and a large family of mutual funds, all with a rare investment perspective of 125 years that spans bull and bear markets, panics, wars, depressions and prosperity.

One William Street

This is one of the Wall Street area's most famous addresses. The Italian Renaissance building was originally built for J. & W. Seligman & Co. in 1907 by Francis Kimball and Julian Levi. Kimball also designed the Trinity and U.S. Realty buildings at 111-115 Broadway. From 1928 to 1980 it was home to Lehman Brothers. There is some irony in this because the Seligmans were always in a league above the Lehmans in spite of the fact that both the Seligmans and the Lehmans came from Bavaria in the 1840s and both set up trading operations in the South. But the Seligmans grew to be one of the most important American banking institutions by the late 1800s and certainly ranked far above Lehman Brothers and Goldman Sachs. After World War I the Lehman firm pushed ahead in all

aspects of banking. Their turn came to rule, and they grew to such an extent that they purchased the land at 85 Broad Street for their new quarters—land that remained vacant, however, during the downturn of the 1970s and was ultimately sold to their competitors, Goldman Sachs.

In 1984 One William Street was substantially renovated and expanded by Gino Valle for its new owner, Banca Commerciale Italiana, for which it received the City Club of New York's Bard Award for Excellence in Architecture and Urban Design in 1988.

The view in the photograph looking down South William's narrow, curving street shows how European many of Wall Street's older buildings seem.

Delmonico's Restaurant

Delmonico's has survived several homes and incarnations; most others, including Luchow's, have succumbed. The original Delmonico's was established in 1827 and offered New Yorkers their first experience in haute cuisine.

Delmonico's building at 56 Beaver Street was designed by James Lord and completed in 1891. It is similar in plan to the famous Flatiron Building, filling an awkward triangular plot formed by two converging streets (Beaver and South William). It is said that the portal behind the porch was brought back from Pompeii by the Delmonico brothers themselves.

At the intersection of William, South William and Beaver Streets, the power and aura of the old financial dis-

trict prevails. The streets are narrow and curved, and the buildings are solid. One William Street and Delmonico's offer graceful corner entrances. Twenty Exchange Place, a slender limestone tower built by Cross & Cross in 1931, offers a rear entrance to this intersection. For many years this building was headquarters to the First Boston Corporation, Kidder Peabody & Co., Shearman & Sterling and Debevoise & Plimpton among others.

Like the private entrances of Dillon Read, Loeb Rhoades and Bache around the corner, these structures remind us, as few other places in the financial district do, how self-assured a world this was and how closed to those who did not meet it on its own terms.

Dillon, Read & Co. Inc.

Here are the old and new entrances of Dillon, Read & Co. Inc., one of Wall Street's most distinguished old-line investment banking firms. Clarence Dillon had joined the firm of William A. Read & Co. as a bond salesman in 1913 and became head of its New York office in 1920. The firm became known as Dillon, Read & Co. the following year. In addition to New York and Chicago, the firm had offices in Boston, Philadelphia, and Paris. Like Morgan Stanley and Kuhn Loeb, the firm concentrated on managerships of offerings rather than participations. During the 1950s it ranked first in the dollar volume of agency private placements.

In the photographs are shown Dillon Read's private entrance at 46 William Street, which it maintained from l948 until l983. Partners and clients were permitted to use this entrance, which had a private, hand-operated elevator car taking them to the upper floors. The rest of the employees used the building's main entrance around the corner at 48 Wall Street (also known as the Bank of New York Building).

When it moved to midtown in 1983, the firm employed the same understated elegance in designing a contemporary entrance plaza.

Today Dillon Read still has only six offices—three in the United States and three abroad—and it maintains its prominence in creative investment banking with the added distinction that it is also known for its gentlemanly conduct. It is frequently the firm that its competitors ask to take on transactions where there are conflicts of interest, because they know they will be handled with first class execution without any of the personality difficulties that can often prevail elsewhere on the Street.

The Shrine of Elizabeth Seton

Located at Seven State Street, this was designed by John McComb and built as a residence for James Watson between 1793 and 1806. Its design is Federal, conforming to the popular style of Washington's early presidency. This is the last of a series of houses that once faced the Battery along State Street, one of the city's most desirable addresses. Built as a gentleman's home, this building demonstrates that even when pressed together in rows, such houses retained elegance and individuality. The unusually slender, elegant Doric columns were actually ship masts. During the Civil War the house was used by the Union Army, which also had an encampment in Battery Park. After the war, it was purchased by Charlotte Grace O'Brien, who upon arriving from Ireland had become disturbed at the treatment of immigrants. She raised $70,000 to purchase the Watson House where she established the Mission of Our Lady of the Rosary to look after the needs of Irish immigrant girls. The Mission still owns the house and maintains it as a shrine to St. Elizabeth Seton.

Mother Seton, born on Staten Island in 1774, was an Episcopalian who converted to Catholicism after her husband's death in 1805. She established the first American congregation of Sisters of Charity, and when canonized in 1971 became America's first saint.

The Trinity Building and Soldiers' Monument

The extraordinarily rich Gothic curtain of this building at 111 Broadway serves as a backdrop to the Trinity Churchyard and the Soldiers' Monument. The building was designed in 1905 by Francis Kimball, who was also responsible for the old United States Trust Co. at 37 Wall Street and the Seligman Building at One William Street.

The Soldiers' Monument was erected in 1852 in memory of the men who were killed during the Revolutionary War and are interred in the Churchyard. They died mostly in British prisons in New York, which remained in British control during most of the war. The internment of the soldiers prevented Trinity Churchyard from being bisected by Albany Street, whose merchants had fought for over forty years, until 1850, to have their street push through and link up with Wall Street. The driving force was the owners of the New York–Albany packets. Four times the extension of Albany Street won municipal approval, but it was never carried out.

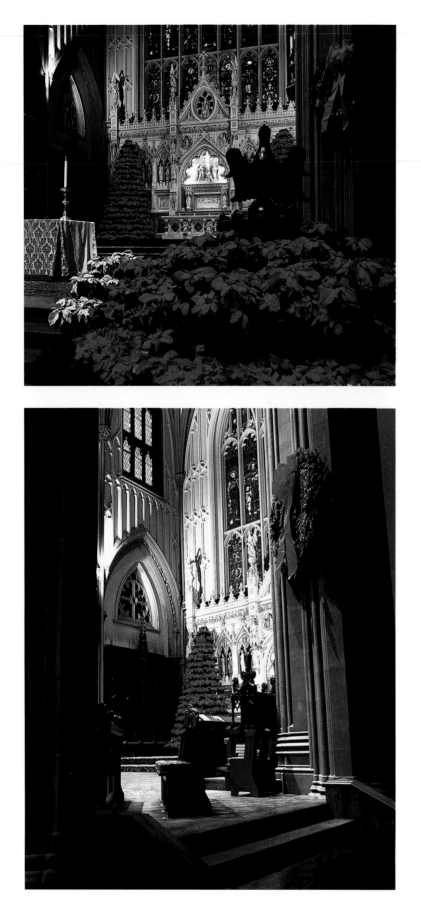

Trinity Church

An oasis of Gothic splendor in the midst of a fast-paced environment, this is the oldest Anglican parish in New York and the third Trinity Church. The first one was built in 1698 and burned in 1776. The second was completed in 1790 with a 200-foot steeple and large Gothic windows. It was deemed structurally unsound and replaced with a new church designed by Richard Upjohn and completed in 1846. The new steeple of 280 feet was the tallest structure in the city for many years.

Trinity marks the beginning of mature Gothic Revival in the United States. The Gothic ribs of late fourteenth century influence, the lancet windows, and the nave arcade all combine to create an uplifting experience. The Christmas poinsettias are among the most magnificent seasonal displays anywhere in New York.

The great chancel window was made on the spot during the construction of the church. It represents some of the oldest stained glass in America and in itself is an innovation, since most of the previous churches had been content with plain glass.

St. Paul's Chapel

This is Manhattan's premier Georgian church, just as Trinity Church is its premier Gothic Revival church. It is also the only pre-Revolutionary building left in New York. There are about twelve other older structures, but these were mostly isolated farmhouses.

The stone for the church is called Manhattan schist and was quarried from the site. Thomas McBean built the church between 1764 and 1766; James Lawrence added the tower and steeple thirty years later. The relatively flat roof of the church is probably responsible for its surviving the great fire of 1776, which destroyed the first Trinity Church and most of the city along Broadway. Members of the congregation were able to stand on St. Paul's roof with pails of water to extinguish the hot embers that blew onto it. This in part explains why St. Paul's is the only building in New York in continuous use that dates from the pre-Revolutionary period.

Originally, the Hudson River extended up to Greenwich Street, creating a pastoral waterfront vista from the western entrance of the church. The churchyard is bound by Vesey Street to the north, named for the Reverend William Vesey, first rector of Trinity Church, and Fulton Street, to the south, named for Robert Fulton, a professional artist. He is also known as the father of the steamship; he built the *Clermont* as well as the first steam warship and the first submarine for the United States Navy.

The elegant interior space of St. Paul's Chapel is created by freestanding Corinthian columns supporting block entablatures. The use of clear windows, Waterford crystal chandeliers and white woodwork—very Georgian and popular in the colonies at the time—results in a bright, cheerful sanctuary. George Washington worshipped here when New York was the nation's capitol and sat to the left of the altar; New York's first governor, George Clinton, sat on the right.

St. Peter's Church

Located at the intersection of Barclay and Church Streets, this church was designed by John Haggerty and Thomas Thomas and completed in 1838, replacing the original structure built in 1786. It is the oldest Roman Catholic parish in New York and the first Catholic church in New York whose exterior follows the Greek Revival style. The interior is of similar spaciousness and grand proportions as the exterior. Above the Baroque altar is a crucifixion scene painted by the Mexican artist José Maria Vallego and donated to the first St. Peter's Church by the New York chargé d'affaires of Charles III of Spain.

In gratitude to the king for his contributions to establishing the first church on this site, the trustees of St. Peter's reserved the front pew in perpetuity for representatives of the Spanish government. The pledge was formally restated in 1976.

The Roman Catholic congregation was formed in 1783 although the first services were held beginning in 1687, during the governorship of Thomas Dongan, who was a Catholic. However, under his successor and thereafter, the Catholic faith was prohibited in the English colonies and services had to be held in private homes. After the Revolutionary War, freedom of religion was established and the first church built by the Catholics was completed here in 1786.

John Street United Methodist Church

Built in 1841 by William Hurry, this is the third Methodist church on this site, where tiny Dutch Street joins John Street. Earlier churches had been constructed in 1768 and 1817. The congregation is the oldest Methodist congregation in the United States. The plain brownstone facade is Greek Revival with the influence of Italianate style; the Palladian window in the center of the facade (a round-topped window flanked by two narrow square-topped windows) is a Northern Italian detail that was popular in England before coming to the United States.

The warm interior of the church has remained unchanged for almost 150 years. It is worth a daily visit just to step back from the pace of the financial district and think about the same area at an earlier time. The church's library contains volumes dating from the 1790s, and its clock, brought over from England in 1767, is still working just fine.

John Street is named for Johannes Haberdinck, a wealthy shoemaker who owned the land that John Street now occupies. During the eighteenth and nineteenth centuries it was inhabited mostly by artisans and craftsmen including a tallow chandler, William Colgate, who later went into manufacturing soap.

"For unto us a child is born.
  unto us a son is given,
And the government will be upon
  his shoulders.
And he will be called
  Wonderful, Counselor, the Mighty God,
  The Everlasting Father, the Prince of Peace."
                                    Isaiah 9:6

American Telephone & Telegraph Building

This magnificent classical structure at 195 Broadway was built in three stages during 1915-22 and was designed by Welles Bosworth.

This is a square-topped layer cake with a deep-set facade of eight Ionic colonnades (each embracing three stories) set atop the row of massive Doric columns depicted in the photograph. This building contains more classical columns than any other facade in the world. The site of the building was that of the Western Union Building, a ten-story structure designed by George Post in 1875. (Post also designed the New York Stock Exchange thirty years later.) Along with the Tribune Building on Park Row, the Western Union Building was one of the first to install elevators. When the building codes were changed in 1892 to permit the steel cage construction without self-supporting walls, significantly taller structures evolved, beginning with the American Surety Company at 100 Broadway in 1895.

The unusual and fascinating lobby of almond marble contains a forest of vast fluted columns with splayed tops. The space is grand and dignified. No flamboyant gestures are needed to remind the visitor that this was the lobby of the largest corporation in the world (with sales of $64.1 billion and assets of $149.5 billion) prior to its reorganization in 1984.

Spirit of Communication

(Opposite) This familiar statue by Evelyn Longman now sits in the lobby of the new American Telephone & Telegraph Company building at 550 Madison Avenue, to which it was moved in 1984. For the previous sixty years it stood atop the round orb *(above)* on the company's former headquarters at 195 Broadway. It also appeared on the covers of telephone directories throughout the country for decades.

Salomon Brothers Inc.

The new headquarters of this firm are at Seven World Trade Center. This building was designed by Emery Roth & Sons who have been responsible for the majority of the waterfront skyscrapers built in the past twenty years. It is best known not for its sleek red granite design but for the last-minute cancellation of its first owner, Drexel Burnham Lambert, Inc., which had become involved in a major securities investigation. At the same time, Salomon Brothers was due to move into an oversized complex at Columbus Circle but also cancelled its plans because of objections raised to the building's extensive mass and also the firm's own internal difficulties. The decision to relocate to Seven World Trade Center has been welcomed by those interested in maintaining the securities industry downtown.

195 Broadway

Christmas lights at the World Trade Center frame this view of the former headquarters of the largest corporation in the world, American Telephone & Telegraph Co. This view from Church Street of its western side shows that the architect ran out of columns. On the other three sides he has assembled a greater collection of columns than appears on any other building constructed in modern times.

A Christmas Present

Christmas of 1913 was very special. Cass Gilbert had presented this architectural gem, called the Woolworth Building, to the city that year. The official opening was April twenty-fourth, when 825 guests assembled for dinner on the twenty-seventh floor and President Wilson threw a switch at the White House that suddenly illuminated eighty thousand electric bulbs. As the orchestra struck up *The Star Spangled Banner*, a telegraphic announcement went out across the ocean to all ships at sea and the Eiffel Tower (the only structure that was taller) that the world's tallest building had opened.

Frank Woolworth's demands (and financial capacity) combined with Cass Gilbert's design to create an extraordinary marriage of Gothic ornamentation with massive scale that is refreshing even today. It is the Mozart of skyscrapers. One of the finest tributes to this great landmark is that its owner and principal tenant is still there, and has kept it in excellent condition, for over seventy-five years. Very few buildings have had such a fate and have remained on top of the critics' list continuously over the years.

The Woolworth Building

The building was christened "The Cathedral of Commerce" by Reverend Parks Cadman, the first of the great radio preachers in the country. He saw the results as an example of faith, exchange, and barter bringing alien people into unity and peace instead of war.

A three-story lobby contains glass mosaics *Commerce* and *Labor (above)*, surrounded by lacy wrought-iron cornices covered with gold leaf. The ceiling is illuminated stained glass, extending over a grand marble staircase that once led to the headquarters of the Irving Bank *(opposite)*.

As Woolworth's competitive juices started flowing he realized that, after assembling the entire real estate block, he could build a structure that would be taller than the nearby Singer Building. He instructed Gilbert to revise the plans many times, ever increasing the size while keeping the gracefulness he had grown to appreciate in the

architect's style. The result is a sixty-story structure finished in terra cotta on all four sides, that remained the tallest building in the world until the Manhattan Bank (40 Wall Street) and Chrysler Buildings were completed in 1930. Because many floors have twenty-foot ceilings, the number of stories in a contemporary building might be about eighty. The golden marble for the lobby was quarried on the Greek Island of Skyros, and Tiffany's supplied the elevator doors.

(Above, left) An amusing touch was provided by sculptor Thomas Johnson: corbels of Cass Gilbert presenting the building and F.W. Woolworth paying for it with nickels and dimes. Frank Woolworth was not a man who believed in leverage. He paid for the building with cash— $13,500,000.

City Hall Park

This was formerly called the Common and lies between Broadway and Park Row, from Vesey to Chambers Streets.

In the early 1700s the City barely extended to Fulton Street, and the eastern edge of the Common (now Park Row) was actually the Boston Post Road.

The Common was officially laid out in about 1730 and surrounds City Hall which was built largely between 1803 and 1812. In 1735 New York's first almshouse was built on the present site of City Hall. In 1842 one of the city's first fountains was installed in the park, to commemorate the completion of the Croton Aqueduct that year, bringing abundant fresh water into the city for the first time. The Croton Reservoir and Aqueduct were hailed as being among the great engineering feats of the nineteenth century. When John Jacob Astor opened his famous Astor House across the street in 1836, he had to dig his own well. That was no problem to Astor, whose 600-bed hotel was larger and grander than any other hotel in London or Paris. It was entirely lit by gaslight, an innovation that some of the guests were not entirely familiar with. On occasion one of them would die peacefully in bed after blowing out the flame before retiring.

City Hall

This building was designed by John McComb and Joseph Mangin, and it was completed in 1812 after nine years of construction.

It is built with elegant white marble and has an usually graceful double flying staircase embracing a circular gallery and central rotunda.

The dome rests on ten Corinthian columns and has a skylight noted for its delicate rosette design.

A major restoration project in the early 1950s has essentially reclad the building and created a structure as sound as the original. The overall design of City Hall is a rare blend of Georgian and French Renaissance; the elegant exterior is duplicated in the grand central hallway.

Lobbies of 111 and 115 Broadway

The entrances are limestone and bronze, the vestibules are Siena marble. The main corridors are a glittering display of marble, bronze, and gold leaf, enhanced by diffused lights and stained glass windows. Each of the lobbies is different and yet they reflect the hand of the same architect, Francis Kimball. No. 111 was completed in 1905 as the Trinity Building and No. 115 in 1907 as the U.S. Realty Building.

Manufacturers Hanover Trust Company

This is the great banking hall of 40 Wall Street, one of the largest commercial banking spaces in New York. Manufacturers Hanover Trust Company is the result of the l961 merger of the Hanover Bank, established in l851, and the Manufacturers Trust Company, which was chartered as the Citizens Trust Company in l905. At the time of its 1961 merger, the bank had more offices in New York than any other bank, and it still does today.

The Equitable Building

At the time of its completion in 1915 this was an extraordinary building. Designed by Ernest Graham and located at 120 Broadway, it contains 1.2 million square feet on a plot of less than an acre. The overwhelmingly massive volume led to New York's and the nation's first comprehensive zoning resolution in 1916—an attempt to regulate the overall height and bulk of buildings in order to assure adequate penetration of light to the streets below. It also limited floor space to twelve times the area of the building's site. The Equitable Building has a floor area almost thirty times the area of its site. The building in-

stalled its own electric generators and even today, during the period of peak electricity demand, Consolidated Edison often asks the building management to fire up its generators to help Con Ed out.

The lobby of the Equitable Building is one of the area's grandest—an ornately coffered barrel vault running the entire block from Broadway to Nassau Street. During the holidays the building's owners provide classical music as an invitation to stop and linger for a few minutes between transactions.

Barclays Bank

The origins of Barclays Bank go back to the 1690s and to one of the goldsmith-bankers of Lombard Street, Joseph Freame. Lombard Street became established at about this time as the London's financial center, so named for the Lombardy region of Italy from which the goldsmiths had originally emigrated in the fourteenth century.

Joseph Freame's sister married James Barclay, and in 1736 he joined the banking partnership. Other family members followed, leading the partnership to take on the Barclays name shortly thereafter. Barclays' worldwide headquarters has been located at the same site on Lombard Street for over two hundred and fifty years.

In the late nineteenth century many small banks felt their size hampered their ability to serve clients and in 1896 Barclays acquired and combined with nineteen other banks to become Barclay and Company Limited. Barclays grew progressively over the next few years, acquiring many banks throughout England and Wales. By 1918 it became one of the "Big Five" English banks. Another acquisition was the Colonial Bank which had already established an agency at 41 Wall Street in 1890. Accordingly, Barclays traces its history in the United States back to 1890, making

it one of the first foreign banks to have a U.S. presence.

Barclays has grown rapidly in America in more recent years. In the late 1970s and early 1980s, the bank expanded its business operations in New York, opened offices in other principal U.S. financial centers, and it acquired business and consumer finance operations. Today nearly thirteen percent of the bank's $189.4 billion in assets are in the United States, making it Barclays' largest commitment outside the United Kingdom. It maintains a network of offices in over seventy countries and ranks as one of the top twenty banks in the world in terms of size. It also operates one of Britain's leading international investment banks.

Today the bank's activities in the United States include wholesale, treasury and capital markets services for large multinational and domestic U.S. companies and institutions, as well as private banking for wealthy individuals. It serves a number of middle market companies located throughout the metropolitan New York area, and it engages in business and consumer finance. As a founding member of the New York Cash Exchange (NYCE), it provides consumer banking to many New Yorkers.

Wall Street's Newcomers: Barclays and Morgan

Two of Wall Street's newest bank buildings are the Barclays Bank Building at 75 Wall Street *(above, left)* and the J.P. Morgan & Co. Building at 60 Wall Street *(above, right)*.

Barclays' building was completed in 1987, designed by Welton Becket Associates. The material is flamed granite, and the lobby is quite lofty. Other British banks have chosen to build on nearby Water Street sites: National Westminster Bank, Standard Chartered Bank, and Lloyds Bank. J. Henry Schroder Wagg was one of the first of the group, moving to the corner of Water and Whitehall Streets in 1969.

The elegant Morgan Building was completed in 1989 and designed by Kevin Roche, John Dinkeloo & Associates. It is distinctive and reminiscent of a classical column.

Kidder, Peabody & Co. Incorporated

The headquarters of this firm have been located at Ten Hanover Square since 1969. This clean structure of the International School was designed by Emery Roth & Sons. The coach lanterns in the foreground are from the India House, which has been a landmark on Hanover Square since 1854, serving as the Cotton Exchange and headquarters of the Hanover Bank and also of W.R. Grace & Company before becoming a luncheon club in 1914.

Kidder, Peabody & Co. Incorporated

Shown here are two of the firm's reception areas, at Hanover Square *(opposite)* and Twenty Exchange Place *(above)*.

Kidder, Peabody was located at Twenty Exchange Place for many years prior to its move to Hanover Square. Old-timers may recognize this scene as having once belonged to another famous tenant: The First Boston Corporation.

Kidder, Peabody & Co. was founded in 1865, probably the oldest major-bracket firm still operating under its original name, and since inception has been a leading investment banking house. It pioneered in the financial development of American Telephone & Telegraph Company and acted as New England manager for a long series of its negotiated underwritten issues.

In the fall of 1930 the firm ran into difficulties due to the decline in prices of securities it owned, the withdrawal of large deposits by the Italian Government and other maturing time deposits. A consortium of banks led by J.P. Morgan, Chase, and First National Bank of Boston extended a credit of $10,000,000. In a later reorganization, Edwin Webster, Jr. (whose father ran Stone & Webster), Chandler Hovey and Albert Gordon stepped in to run the firm. Additional personnel joined in 1935 when the securities affiliates of Chase, National City Bank, and Guaranty Trust Company were closed as mandated by the Glass-Steagall Act.

Under the active leadership of Albert Gordon, Kidder, Peabody was able to restore its business and continue to grow in all areas. The partners and employees sought all types of investment banking business: managerships if they could be obtained and otherwise participations. No issue

was too small for them, no participation too insignificant. In addition to its principal offices in New York, Boston, and Philadelphia, it opened offices in Chicago, then in Hartford and Albany. From its standing in 1931, with practically no business at all, it moved up to the top in the number of issues managed within twenty-five years.

Today, Kidder, Peabody ranks among the leading global investment banking and brokerage firms with assets in excess of $20 billion, due in part to its 1986 sale of an eighty percent interest to GE Financial Services, a unit of General Electric Company. The firm provides a full range of client services: merchant banking, investment banking, mergers & acquisitions advisory services, asset finance, and institutional and individual investment services with a heritage and vision unique among today's Wall Street firms.

(Above) One of Wall Street's great patriarchs is Albert Gordon who arrived at Kidder, Peabody as a partner in 1931. He was one of three senior partners of the firm until it incorporated in 1962. He was then elected chairman and chief executive officer, a position he held until 1986, when he became honorary chairman. An avid walker, he often walked to Wall Street from his home on Gracie Square and recently was running the London marathons. Mr. Gordon's personal rapport with his clients is legendary. No one had to wait long for a return phone call no matter where he was, whether traveling through Kansas or Kenya.

55 Wall Street

(Opposite) Presently a Citibank branch and formerly the headquarters of First National City Bank, this was originally the Merchants' Exchange. It was built between 1836 and 1842, designed by Isaiah Rogers, and converted to the United States Custom House in 1863 by William Potter. It was remodeled during 1905-07 and doubled in height by McKim, Mead & White. The latter performed excellent architectural surgery when they added a huge Corinthian colonnade to an equally huge Ionic colonnade that had been built sixty-five years before.

McKim, Mead & White did not duplicate what had been done; they added their own interpretation—Corinthian versus Ionic, using similar proportions and emphasis on depth and shadow. The portico contains twelve granite columns rising forty feet and screening an enormous, recessed three-story porch. An interesting interlude is thus created between these massive columns and the main entrance.

The interior is one of Wall Street's grandest. It has had many incarnations, even during Citibank's reign, from a hushed collection of lending officers sitting at mahogany desks to a more contemporary environment of tellers and machines.

Shearman & Sterling, one of the city's oldest and largest law firms, was located in this building before moving uptown in 1987. It chose to have its own private entrance at 53 Wall Street.

Wall Street Plaza

(Above) Also known as the Eighty-eight Pine Street Building, this is one of I.M. Pei's most significant in New York—a white, crisp and elegant building and one of the first to have butted glass filling the entire structural bays without the use of mullions. Together with Skidmore, Owings & Merrill's 140 Broadway this is one of the area's classiest new buildings. It was completed in 1973 and is presently owned by the Orient Overseas Association.

Thirty-three Maiden Lane

(Above) This was originally intended to be an annex to the Federal Reserve Bank, and architects Philip Johnson and John Burgee attempted to duplicate some of the latter's style in 1983. It is now an office building, whose massive foyer with tall distinctive windows are a refreshing break on crowded Nassau Street. The name Maiden Lane derives from the Dutch *Maagde Paetje*, a path alongside a pebbly brook that ran from Nassau Street to the East River. The brook was where the washing was done—a chore assigned to the young girls in most families.

Continental Center

(Opposite) This large structure at 180 Maiden Lane contains one million square feet and has an unusual greenhouse entrance. It was designed by Swanke, Hayden, Connell & Partners and completed in 1983. It is headquarters to Continental Insurance Company and also Nomura Securites International, Inc.

The Continental Insurance Company was organized in New York in 1853 at a time when there was greater concern for fire insurance than life insurance. Given the prevalence of candles, oil lamps and wood-burning fireplaces, major cities around the country were continuously exposed to fires.

The city had no full-time fire department. It was forced to rely on volunteers who were organized into companies in which membership was mainly social. Insurance companies customarily paid a reward to the volunteer brigade that saved the building they insured. Oval, rectangular

and diamond-shaped metal fire marks attached to a building indicated which company insured it. Great rivalry existed among the neighborhood companies, so that fires were fought more out of sport than from any sense of commitment. Competition reached such a degree that actual firefighting became secondary to arriving first on the scene to collect the reward.

On December 8, 1852 a group of businessmen met to propose the formation of Continental for the purpose of furnishing reliable insurance protection for the community, including, hopefully, the staying power to withstand future calamities which often sent existing insurers into bankruptcy. As required by law, the books for subscription to the company's stock were publicly offered. Within two hours more than $500,000 had been spoken for, the largest amount of capital yet subscribed by any New York insurance company. Its shares were listed some years later on the New York Stock Exchange.

In its first year of operation, Continental began to experiment with the use of agents to expand its business outside the city. Until then all insurers inspected their customers' properties personally. Also that year, it stated a dividend policy of allowing shareholders to participate in the firm's profits, provided they also participated to the same extent in its losses. Continental's first dividend was declared and paid on July 18, 1853, and it has continued to pay dividends to the present day without interruption.

Over the years Continental has offered innovative insurance policies, taking it far afield from its original lines. It has grown internally and through acquisitions, and this handsome new office building on the shores of the East River attests to its accomplishments during the past 140 years.

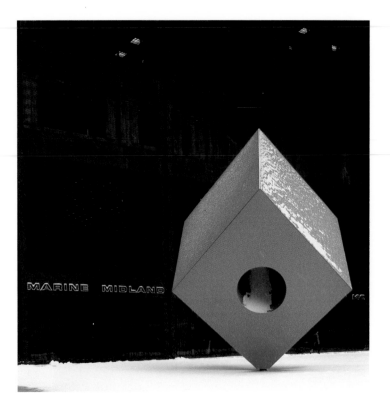

The Red Cube

Isamu Noguchi designed this bright red cube in 1967, placed it on its end with a hole down the middle, and set it next to the dark bronze glass facade of the Marine Midland Bank tower. The cube is technically a rhombohedron —a six-sided figure whose opposite sides are parallel at oblique angles. This element of disharmony creates a field of energy around the sculpture.

The Marine Midland Bank Building at 140 Broadway was designed by Skidmore, Owings & Merrill and built in 1967. Lever House may have been Skidmore, Owings & Merrill's most influential building in New York, but 140 Broadway is considered its best. The glass curtain wall is dark, refined, and discreet, resulting in a soft feeling in spite of its glass and steel construction. The building is irregular in shape, conforming to its plot rather than defying it. The red Noguchi cube gently balanced on one corner further adds to the gentleness of this building.

Marine Midland Banks, Inc. was founded in Buffalo on Lake Erie in 1850 to provide financing and trade arrangements for Great Lakes grain shippers. The bank expanded its growth along the Erie Canal and the railroad lines into the "Midlands" of New York State, which accounts for the second part of its name.

Today, Marine Midland has headquarters in both New York City and Buffalo, and it is one of the twenty-five largest banks in the country. Affiliated with the Hongkong Bank Group, it is taking advantage of expanding opportunities in American-Asian finance and trade.

Double Check

(Opposite) This bronze statue by J. Seward Johnson was commissioned in 1982 by Merrill Lynch, which had occupied the offices directly across from it on Liberty Street. The figure is reading a memo on Merrill Lynch letterhead. His briefcase contains a calculator, tape recorder, pencils and occasionally an actual sandwich provided by passers-by.

Merrill Lynch was the primary tenant at One Liberty Plaza, which was built by the U.S. Steel Corporation in 1970. It replaced the famous Singer Building, designed by Ernest Flagg and completed in 1908. At forty-one stories, this was the tallest building in New York ever demolished and is considered the city's greatest loss since Penn Station. The tower was illuminated at night and had its own generator for heat, light and power for its elevators. It also had a central vacuum-cleaning system which included a special set of pipes for cleaning top hats. Flagg built the building in the manner of his clients' products: solid and reliable—never to wear out. When completed, he thought the Singer Building would be as "solid and lasting as the Pyramids." He was off on his timing, but to his credit at least the building took four times longer to demolish than its new replacement took to complete.

When One Liberty Plaza was completed, its principal tenants were Merrill Lynch, Pierce, Fenner & Smith and White, Weld & Co. A third primary tenant, Blyth & Co., did not move in as originally planned but moved in with Eastman, Dillon & Co. at One Chase Manhattan Plaza instead. When Merrill Lynch acquired White Weld in 1978 a number of executives of the latter firm never changed offices—just their stationery and calling cards.

Donaldson, Lufkin & Jenrette, Inc.

In 1959 three classmates from Harvard Business School, in their mid-thirties, decided to leave their respective firms, join forces and create a new one. This was a bold move, because they decided not to create a specialty boutique but a full-line investment banking organization.

Further pioneering efforts occurred in 1969 when Donaldson, Lufkin & Jenrette, already a New York Stock Exchange member, decided to go public. Since only First Boston had any public ownership, Donaldson, Lufkin & Jenrette decided to appoint them as manager of its offering, which was brought to market in April 1970. Prior to this time no Exchange member firms were allowed to be publicly owned, which explains why First Boston did not have its own seat until 1971. Donaldson, Lufkin's pioneering efforts, which the Exchange did not view very sympathetically at the time, are largely responsible for the tide of equity capital raised subsequently by Merrill Lynch, Reynolds & Co., Paine Webber, Dean Witter and others during the early 1970s.

The firm has built its reputation on six strong bases: imaginative corporate finance (including high yield bonds), merchant banking, venture capital (Sprout Group), research, asset management (Wood Struthers), and correspondent brokerage (Pershing).

Until the early 1980s, DLJ, as the firm is known, was highly dependent on equities-related businesses, stemming in large part from its excellence in research and venture capital. In fact its twenty-year-old Sprout Group currently has a portfolio of investments in over fifty new companies aggregating approximately $138 million. Over the years DLJ has continued to pioneer, developing an expertise in investment and merchant banking. It has established a $1 billion bridge fund to provide support to its clients in merchant banking activities. In this area DLJ is able to bring its reputation for the creativity, flexibility and personal attention typically associated with an investment banking boutique but with a staff of over 130 professionals and an institutional distribution and capital-raising capability equivalent to those of the largest firms.

In the fast lanes of today's financial markets the personal satisfaction of a firm's employees is often overlooked. DLJ takes the opposite approach and even lists "having fun" as one of its corporate objectives.

It employs approximately 1,300 in its downtown offices, surrounded by the Street's most extraordinary collection of early American art.

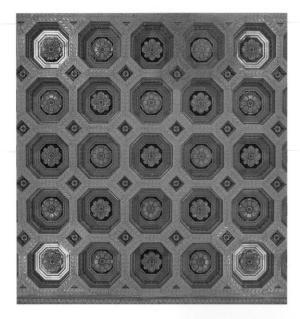

A Wall Street Quiz

Anyone who can identify the offices shown on these and the following four pages without first looking at the identifying captions may now take early retirement.

The famous Bankers' Club shown here at 120 Broadway was located on the thirty-eighth floor of what was then the tallest building in the world. When it opened in 1915 this was the greatest of the downtown luncheon clubs. My grandfather was a charter member, having transferred over from the Lawyers' Club across the street.

Since it was a new club in an unusually large building,

the Bankers' Club decided to do everything on a massive scale. The entrance foyer pictured here is larger than most suburban homes. There were four dining rooms, among which the Oak Room is shown here, during its occupancy by Tucker, Anthony & R.L. Day. Donaldson, Lufkin &

Jenrette has taken the Grill Room, while Lester, Schwab, Katz & Dwyer occupies the rest.

The Bankers' Club closed its doors in 1979, a victim of the market downturn at the time.

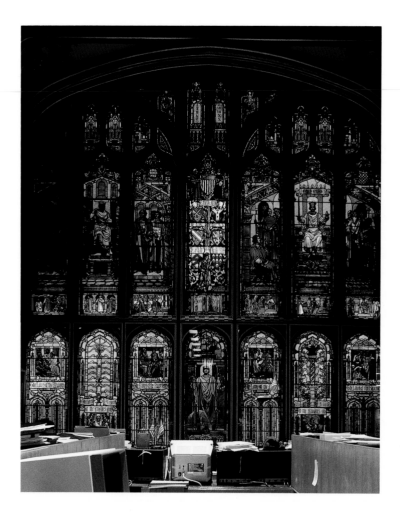

The Lawyers' Club

This club was located at 115 Broadway and is now headquarters for the New York Stock Exchange member firm and specialist, Spear, Leeds & Kellogg, Inc.

Organized in 1887, the Lawyers' Club was once one of the oldest and best known downtown luncheon clubs in New York. It was originally located in the old Equitable Building at 120 Broadway. After the Equitable Building burned in 1912, the club was completely destroyed and it relocated to the upper three floors at 115 Broadway. (In 1918, Thomas Masaryk was speaking at the Lawyers' Club when he received a cable that he had been chosen president of the new nation of Czechoslovakia.) The main dining hall was described as one of the most beautiful in the country, two stories in height with a stained glass window representing the history of law, designed by J. Gordon Guthrie. This beautiful window had a fountain below, giving the room an atmosphere quite unlike that of any other club.

Unfortunately, the club went out of business in 1979 and remained empty until Spear, Leeds & Kellogg acquired the space in 1982 and has carefully refurbished it to its original splendor. The main dining hall is now a trading room with the famous stained glass window remaining intact. The entrance lobby remains much the same as in the days of the original club and the old members' lounge is now Spear, Leeds & Kellogg's floor members' room.

Spear, Leeds & Kellogg was established in 1933 by Harold Spear, Lawrence Leeds and James Kellogg III (who became chairman of the New York Stock Exchange in 1941). The firm is the largest specialist on both the New York and the American Stock Exchanges, making markets in 130 and 100 stocks, respectively. Its affiliate, Troster, Singer & Co. trades five thousand stocks over the counter.

Rockefeller and Morgan

Here are the inner sancta of Wall Street's two most influential men: John D. Rockefeller *(above)* and J.P. Morgan *(opposite)*.

When he was chairman of the Standard Oil Company, Rockefeller maintained an office on the twenty-first floor of this building at 26 Broadway. It is designed in an elaborate Tudor style with mahogany beams dissecting a decorative ceiling, all supported by massive stone walls with arched windows. It is pure fantasy, but the owner could have whatever he chose, and an English castle seemed appropriate to him at the time.

J.P. Morgan selected a pyramid on the top of the Bankers Trust Building at 14 Wall Street for his residence while his own building was under construction at 23 Wall Street. Of great influence in banking circles, he was not as wealthy as some thought. In fact, when he died in 1913 and left an estate valued at just over $100 million, Rockefeller commented, "And to think, he wasn't even a rich man."

Today Rockefeller's offices are occupied by Carr Securities Corporation and Morgan's residence by La Tour d'Or restaurant.

Upstairs at the New York Stock Exchange

(Above) The Exchange's main board room is magnificent to an extent beyond almost any other American corporation including the powerful Federal Reserve Bank of New York. There are twenty-seven chairs at the thirty-five-foot-long table, each with a director's name plate on the back. The portraits are all of past governors, and the tall clock and president's podium used to be on the floor of the Exchange in the last century.

(Opposite) The Exchange's Members' Lunch Club is located on the seventh floor of its building. Since 1903 members have enjoyed the convenience of dining upstairs in a more quiet atmosphere than typically prevails on the floor. Like the Downtown Association, this is a lunch club whose future is assured and which is in no hurry to change with the latest trends. Its menus are basically the same as they were in the 1940s.

141

The Floor of the New York Stock Exchange

The floor of the NYSE is one of the most active in the world by day. At night it is a different scene. A system of conduits for electronic cables now extends into the vast interior space above the floor. Prior to this, large annunciator boards on each side of the floor would flash a broker's number calling him to his trading post, which may have given the Exchange the nickname of "the Big Board."

The evolution of the New York Stock Exchange began in 1869, although its trading association stretches all the way back to 1792. Continuous trading of stocks throughout the day, rather than only during the morning and afternoon roll calls, began in 1873 with some brokers dealing in particular stocks at one location on the trading floor instead of wandering about. Two technological inventions were crucial to the Exchange: Morse's telegraph (1844), which provided quick communications between brokers and investors throughout the country, and the stock ticker (1867), which replaced the messenger boys, known as "pad shovers," who constantly ran (often late) between the trading floors and brokers' offices. By 1880 the telephone replaced the telegraph and enabled trading volume to reach into the millions by 1900. The first million-share day was in 1886, but this became more frequent in the early part of the next century, fueled by the growth of the railroads and the trusts.

Trading volume exceeded three million shares for the first time just before its move into greatly expanded facilities in 1903. The new trading floor was one of the grandest spaces in the nation, with marble walls, generous dimensions, an ornate gilt ceiling, 79 feet high and the famous annunciator boards.

In mid-October (a favorite panic month) of 1907 there was a run on banks and stock prices began to fall. The precipitous decline was halted through the intervention of J.P. Morgan, who organized a consortium of major banks to subscribe over $25 million to hold up the market. The panic was halted by mid-November. This was the last time that one man could command the financial resources adequate to change the course of an unfavorable market. The era of the market titans and speculators came to an end with World War I.

A bull market ensued after the war, due to the expansion of the United States' consumer market and its emergence as a creditor to Europe. New York replaced London as the center of international finance, and during the next decade, over 1700 foreign issues were offered publicly in the United States. With the growth in personal income came the cash available for investment, and popular interest directed these funds into the stock market. Annual trading volume increased from 450 million shares in 1925 to over one billion in 1929. When the market crashed on October 29, 1929 over 16 million shares were traded, a record not surpassed for thirty-nine years. Much of the panic derived from the breakdown in communications and the long delays in the ticker's ability to report prices.

After that, high-speed tickers were installed and computers replaced the pneumatic tube system. By April 1968 trading volume surpassed the 1929 record for the first time, and brokers who had not adequately automated their back offices were awash in the paperwork crisis. The Exchange was forced to curtail trading hours and ultimately had to arrange the sale of Goodbody & Co. to Merrill Lynch lest the former's collapse bring down the entire system. By 1973 member firms' back offices were under control, and the Exchange introduced the fully automated Designated Order Turnaround ("DOT") system to route electronically small orders and reports between member firms and the NYSE. Later systems speeded processing of market orders received before the opening and made processing of limit orders easier. One of the great credits to the New York Stock Exchange was that during the high volume and uncertain days of October 19-20, 1987, the NYSE market system continued to function, preventing, with the assistance of the Federal Reserve Bank, more serious repercussions. As a result of studies following the October 1987 market break, the NYSE undertook close to 30 initiatives designed to strengthen its market system. Among them: increased volume capacity; accelerated routing of individual investors' small orders through its SuperDOT System during active and volatile markets; and an agreement with the Chicago Mercantile Exchange on various circuit-breaker procedures to provide cooling-off periods in times of extreme volatility.

The American Stock Exchange

The origins of the American Stock Exchange ("the AMEX") are colorful and equally as modest as the beginnings of the New York Stock Exchange. The latter began as a trading forum under a buttonwood tree while the AMEX started at the curbstone on Broad Street near Exchange Place. Nothing stopped the curb brokers; even in the snow and rain they gathered around the lamp posts and mail boxes, putting up lists of stocks for sale. By 1900, millions of dollars' worth of securities in mining companies, farm machinery, railroads, life insurance, and printing and textile companies were being traded in the street. With the increase of volume, the more enterprising brokers rented rooms above the street, where their clerks could receive telephone orders and call them down to the curb. This worked fine until the level of shouting reached such an extent that special broker hand signals were substituted, a system that has prevailed on the AMEX for decades after it moved indoors.

In 1921 the New York Curb Market, as it was called, moved inside. In 1929 it became the New York Curb Exchange and moved to new expanded facilities at 78 Trinity Place in 1931. It was not until 1953 that it officially became the American Stock Exchange.

Today a listing on the AMEX affords companies greater liquidity, visibility and analyst coverage, resulting in an increased propensity for major institutions to hold its shares. Another benefit is the national recognition, which is measured by the marked increase in the number of large brokerage firms holding shares for their accounts. The AMEX also provides ongoing services to its listed clients, including the access of several thousand retail brokers and portfolio managers through its worldwide luncheon meeting clubs, industry seminars and conferences. It also prepares a bi-monthly report for investment professionals focusing on a different group of listed companies in each issue. The AMEX is also setting in motion the necessary steps that will enable it to double its peak-trading capacity by the end of 1989.

Christmas Eve

" 'Twas the night before Christmas, and all through the house, not a creature was stirring, not even a mouse." Trading terminals at one of the foreign securities firms are decorated for an American Christmas.

The New York Mercantile Exchange

(Opposite) This is one of five commodities exchanges sharing close quarters at the World Trade Center. It is the most successful of the group and the oldest—founded in 1872 as a market for agricultural products. It diversified into platinum futures in 1956 and palladium in 1968. The demand for these high-technology metals, plus the introduction of oil futures in 1978, has enabled the Merc, which is also today referred to as the NYMEX, to become the fastest-growing futures exchange in the United States. Since 1980 its trading volume has grown at an average annual rate of over fifty percent to a projected 1989 volume of over 40 million contracts. It is the only futures exchange in the country devoted exclusively to pricing, hedging and trading essential industrial commodities.

Platinum and palladium are the most widely used of a group of six metals that includes rhodium, ruthenium, osmium and iridium. Their unique chemical and physical qualities make them vital industrial materials. Over fifty percent of the United States demand for platinum for example is due to its use in automotive catalytic converters. Palladium is now replacing gold in electrical and electronic contacts and semiconductors.

The NYMEX added heating oil futures contracts in 1978, followed by gasoline, crude oil and propane. Options on crude oil futures began in 1986, followed by heating oil and gasoline futures in 1987 and 1989, respectively. Current trading activity in the energy futures complex is the equivalent of 130 million barrels of oil per day.

Membership in the NYMEX is divided into 816 "seats" which are owned by individuals representing brokerage interests in commodities, and personal trading interests.

147

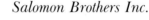

Salomon Brothers Inc.

Salomon Brothers & Co. was formed in January, 1910 as a partnership of three brothers (Arthur, Herbert and Percy) plus a clerk, Benjamin Levy, to continue their father's business of money brokerage. The firm was long on ambition but short on capital, and in April of that year had to merge with Martin Hutzler & Co. because the latter had a seat on the New York Stock Exchange, which Salomon Brothers could not afford.

But the principal activity of the firm was issuing and trading bonds, whose importance during the early part of the century eclipsed that of equities in the raising of new capital funds. The issuers were American railroads and other corporations as well as foreign governments. The United States Government was absent from the capital markets because its expenditures were modest and it had no deficit. The firm's clients were financial institutions and trusts who were generally required to invest only in bonds. Starting first with bankers' acceptances, the firm moved into rail equipment trust certificates, tax anticipation notes, federal land bank notes, and foreign currency obligations. It became one of the first primary dealers in government paper, and in 1922 it moved its headquarters to 60 Wall Street, with branch offices in Boston, Chicago, Philadelphia, Minneapolis and Cleveland.

There were numerous big bond firms with lots of capital, but none ventured as far as Salomon to the extent of its market making. Salomon always made a market in everything it sold and was the one firm where a bid for a debt instrument could be obtained. By the 1950s bond offerings were considered unsalable if Salomon would not touch them. Being outside of Wall Street's establishment, the firm broke the "capital strike" in 1935 with an offering of first mortgage bonds for Swift & Co. The boycott had been created by the issuing houses as a protest to Joseph Kennedy's tough new SEC regulations. Most public offerings were turned into private placements. Salomon went ahead anyway and earned grudging respect by the other houses. Still it needed more origination business and in 1962 it teamed up with Merrill Lynch, Lehman Brothers and Blyth & Co. to form "the Fearsome Foursome" to get more competitive bidding opportunities. In the mid-1960s it began to transfer its institutional relationships to stocks as well as bonds and became a major player in block trading.

For decades the historical syndicates were considered to be absolutely sacrosanct. Once a firm was in a particular syndicate as a major, it was a major for life. Dillon Read and Kuhn Loeb were in a special bracket that excluded others who felt they were more capable. The landmark issue that broke all historical ties came in 1979 when IBM Corporation replaced its traditional lead manager, Morgan Stanley, with Salomon Brothers and Merrill Lynch. Morgan Stanley was in part responsible because of its policy not to have co-managers or to appear in tombstones unless it was first. In one stroke the IBM deal simply said that companies were free to choose their own investment bankers and not be dominated by historical circumstances. John Gutfreund is credited with laying the groundwork. During the 1960s he would call up the major firms such as Dillon Read in the midst of a large debt offering and simply buy a major portion of the transaction. The bonds were sold and gradually major corporations realized the tremendous placing capacity of Salomon.

Barely noticed in the 1950s, Salomon was instrumental in helping to save New York City from bankruptcy in 1975 and the Chrysler Corporation in 1980. The latter's deficit exceeded $1 billion in 1979 and it had run out of all available funds. Salomon coordinated a rescue plan that included unprecedented federal loan guarantees of $1.5 billion.

From 1981 until 1986 it had a stormy marriage with Phibro Corp. (née Philipp Brothers) which ended in divorce. Salomon Brothers always was, and remains today, a loose federation of independent traders and salesmen, cooperating more like a medieval guild than a structured corporation.

In 1970 the firm moved to One New York Plaza and created the largest private trading floor in the world, commonly referred to as "the room." The Hutzler name was dropped that year when the firm reverted to its original Salomon Brothers. It opened offices in London in 1971 and Tokyo in 1980 so that it now maintains round-the-clock trading activities with a portfolio of approximately $11 billion, adhering to one of Arthur Salomon's principal tenets, to stand prepared to repurchase whatever is sold.

Wall Street Patriarchs

The Bankers Trust Building (1912), designed by Trowbridge & Livingston, and to its right the Equitable Building (1915), designed by Ernest Graham, are two of Wall Street's most famous landmarks. At the time of its completion, the Bankers Trust Company Building was considered the world's tallest structure (540 feet) on so small a plot (94 by 97 feet). J.P. Morgan took up residence in the pyramid, long the bank's logo, to watch construction of his own building at 23 Wall Street, designed by the same architect. The bank subsequently acquired three properties adjacent to 16 Wall Street—Fourteen Wall Street and Seven Pine Street, both in 1917, and Fifteen Pine Street in 1927. All three were replaced by a 25-story structure

that year which had floor levels matching 16 Wall Street, abutting the latter on the west and south, producing internally a single building covering the eastern half of the block bounded by Wall, Nassau and Pine Streets and Broadway.

The Equitable Building was simply the largest building in the world when it opened in 1915. This photograph is taken from the location of the Curb Exchange on Broad Street, approximately where the original canal stopped. Outdoor trading began in 1865 and continued until 1921 when the brokers moved to indoor quarters on Trinity Place.

Drexel Burnham Lambert, Inc.

This is the firm's principal New York office at 60 Broad Street. Drexel & Co. was organized in 1940, using the name and facilities of the Philadelphia branch of Drexel Morgan & Co. The original Drexel & Co. was established in 1837 and was affiliated with J.P. Morgan from 1871 until 1940. Drexel & Co. became known as Drexel, Harriman Ripley & Co. and then Drexel, Firestone & Co., Inc. in 1971 with the infusion of capital from the Firestone family. In 1973 it merged with Burnham & Company, Inc., a firm that had opened in 1935 and was known for its

trading and brokerage capabilities.

In 1976 Drexel Burnham Group Inc. merged with Lambert Brussels Witter, forming the present firm. Compagnie Brussels Lambert had started in 1840 and by 1970, when it acquired William D. Witter, Inc. as one of its first U.S. investments, it had become Belgium's second largest holding company.

Today the firm employs over six thousand people in thirty-one offices and has gained a reputation for innovative financing using less-than-investment-grade debt securities.

Liberty Tower

(Above) This tower at 55 Liberty Street was designed by Henry Ives Cobb and constructed between 1909 and 1910. For many years this was the headquarters of the Sinclair Oil Company which was acquired by British Petroleum in 1969. The design is one of the first to expand on the newly approved steel cage construction and create a unified rather than tripartite system of composition. The highly ornamental Gothic exterior is created with terra cotta, a technique later used by Cass Gilbert at 90 West Street and on the Woolworth Building.

Architectural Extravaganza

(Opposite) This experience exists only downtown, with its irregular streets and mixture of structures of different centuries. Take a moment to savor the variety because they represent a rich selection of different styles.

In the foreground are buildings constructed along Pearl Street from 1829 to 1858 on what was New York's first landfill. To the left is the massive Goldman Sachs Building, with J.P. Morgan's distinctive new classical column in the center. In front of J.P. Morgan, reflected in the puddle, is the columned facade of the W.R. Grace & Co. Building. Between Morgan and a new red brick office building at Seven Hanover Square is the Cities Service Building (1932), now known as the American International Building.

One Wall Street

(Above) This shimmering limestone tower, designed by Ralph Walker in 1932, is skyscraping at its best— massive and yet finely detailed. It is a fitting companion to Trinity Church whose chapel roof I have captured in the foreground.

The building was built for the Irving Trust Company, which was founded in 1851 and named for Washington Irving. The bank's previous headquarters were in the Woolworth Building before moving to One Wall Street in 1932. The bank was acquired by the Bank of New York in 1989.

100 Broadway

(Opposite) The American Surety Building was designed by Bruce Price and completed in 1895, with an extension in 1921 by Herman Lee Meade and a renovation in 1975 by Kajima International.

This is one of Wall Street's loveliest buildings in every respect. At its base is a colonnade of massive Ionic columns on which stand a row of full-sized classical figures. The elaborate multistoried cornice on the top projects six feet. When completed not only was this the tallest build-

ing in the world, it was also the most admired. It was built by the American Surety Company for its headquarters as one of the country's major surety companies. Transamerica Corporation acquired the company in 1947 and the Bank of Tokyo acquired the building in 1974, making careful renovations to enable it to last another hundred years.

In the 1870s New York had a series of tall buildings (Equitable Life—1871, Western Union—1875, and the Tribune Building—1875) called "elevator buildings." They all still had heavy masonry walls. In 1892 the city adopted a change in its building codes that permitted the steel cage construction (Chicago was first—in the 1880s). This important modification permitted the development of the modern skyscraper as we know it today, with 100 Broadway being one of the earliest examples in New York—the center of skyscraper development for the past century.

Wall Street Canyons

(Above) From the corner of Hanover Square one can see the classical spire and eagle on top of the Bank of New York Building at 48 Wall Street. This tasteful Renaissance Revival building was designed in 1929 by Benjamin Morris, who also is known for the Cunard Line Building. The Bank of New York's rich upper stories are stepped back and contain a Greek temple, a tower to the west of the temple, and an eagle atop the tower.

(Opposite) The Trinity Building, 111 Broadway (1905) and the U. S. Realty Building, 115 Broadway (1907), were both designed by Francis Kimball.

These magnificent long and narrow structures were built by Harry Black of the George Fuller Construction Company. Their rich Gothic facades harmonize with Trinity Church and glow in the late afternoon sun. The famous Lawyers' Club, one of Wall Street's oldest luncheon clubs, was located atop the U.S. Realty Building, and Goodbody & Co. was on lower floors. Those who remember this spot will also recall that one of Brooks Brothers' first branches in the country was located on the ground floor of the Trinity Building.

One day a colleague of mine was invited to dine with his uncle at the Lawyers' Club and had mistakenly gone to the top of the wrong building. Because he was running late, he decided to try the open catwalk connecting the two buildings rather than retrace his steps. The rusting bridge was on its last legs with loose or missing planks. My friend finally made it to the other side and stumbled into the Lawyers' Club kitchen, a bit shaken. His appetite was temporarily sated from the experience.

Wall Street from Washington Street

(*Opposite*) This view of the financial district is from the Downtown Athletic Club's Washington Street entrance. From the left in the photograph are No. Two World Trade Center, One Bankers Trust Plaza, Nineteen Rector Street, Two Rector Street with the Port Authority parking garage in the foreground, One Liberty Street with the elegant Trinity Building in its foreground, and Nos. 71 to 39 Broadway.

Beginning TriBeCa

(*Above*) This is the view of Wall Street from its northern edge, TriBeCa. Residences have sprouted along Greenwich Street serving the financial district, especially the World Financial Center and the World Trade Center. The term TriBeCa derives from the triangular-shaped area below Canal Street.

The American Express Building

(*Above*) This is the firm's former headquarters at 65 Broadway, completed in 1917 and designed by Renwick, Aspinwall & Tucker. It was also home for many years to J. & W. Seligman & Co. after they moved from One William Street. American Express was formed in 1850 and occupied different locations on Wall Street and lower Broadway until 1874 when it moved to old 65 Broadway, the site of the present structure that replaced the earlier one in 1917. Prior to its demolition, American Express acquired old 65 Broadway in 1902 for $2.2 million, the largest private cash real estate transaction ever negotiated in New York up to that time.

After American Express moved to 125 Broad Street the building became headquarters to the American Bureau of Shipping and in 1989 was acquired as the new headquarters of J.J. Kenny & Co. The graceful 21-story building is designed in an H-plan with light-filled courtyards on both sides connected with an enclosed arcade on the upper floors.

Nos. 71, 65 and 61 Broadway

(*Opposite*) These handsome structures were built as follows: 71 Broadway, completed in 1894 and designed by Renwick, Aspinwall & Tucker. It was known as the Empire Building and was home to the U.S. Steel Corporation for many years. At 65 Broadway is the American Express Company Building, built by the Aspinwall firm in 1917. Next door is 61 Broadway, completed in 1916 and designed by Francis Kimball for Adams Express Co. It was also home to J. Henry Schroder Bank & Trust Co. until their relocation to One State Street in 1969. Presently Ingalls & Snyder is headquartered here, among other firms.

This section of Broadway is believed to be the site of the original structures put up in 1613 by Captain Adriaen Block. He had come to America seeking to profit from the beaver-fur trade. In November of that year his ship accidentally caught fire and burned down to the waterline. With no other means of returning to the Netherlands, Block and his crew set up their winter camp on the hill near Exchange Place. With the assistance of the natives, they built four small shelters and became the first colonists.

One Hundred Broadway

(*Above*) These three Greek goddesses (including stern-faced Prudence holding a mirror) are from a series of life-sized figures on top of the colonnade at 100 Broadway. They are by J. Massey Rhind, a noted sculptor at the turn of the century and were installed in 1895. Rhind is also known for his massive frieze on the South Wall of Alexander Hall at Princeton University.

America

(*Opposite*) This is one of *The Four Continents* at the U.S. Custom House by the sculptor Daniel Chester French (1903-1907).

French is best known for his statue of Abraham Lincoln at Washington's Lincoln Memorial. The collection of four continents at the U.S. Custom House is the most celebrated of his sculptures in New York, and it is perhaps the one he took the greatest pride in.

America is depicted by a woman of the pioneering days, an abundant sheaf of corn (representing material prosperity) across her lap. Her right hand holds the torch of liberty and enlightenment. At her left side Mercury sets in motion the winged wheels of commerce—a straightforward reference to America's growing industrial power at the beginning of the twentieth century.

163

John Watts

(*Above, left*) He was the last Royal Recorder of the City of New York and died in 1836. This statue was erected in Trinity Churchyard by his grandson, James Watts de Peyster in 1893.

John Wolfe Ambrose

(*Above, right*) This sculpture of Ambrose (1838-1899) was completed by Andrew O'Connor in 1899 and is presently installed on the south side of the Battery Park concession building. One of the financial district's many unsung heros

is John Ambrose, an engineer, who is largely responsible for transforming New York from just another shipping town into the greatest port city in the world.

For more than forty years, Ambrose fought for Congressional support of his plan to widen the shipping channel into New York. The plan cut the distance into the port by six miles, and the wider, deeper channel allowed access by the larger ships. The *Ambrose* lightship guided vessels approaching the channel from 1908 until 1963. It has been part of the South Street Seaport since 1968.

Those with good eyes will notice a pigeon hatching her family under the protection of Mr. Ambrose's flamboyant whiskers.

U.S. Steel Corporation

(*Above, left*) This is one of four of U.S. Steel Corporation's eagles at 71 Broadway. The building was originally known as the Empire Building, built in 1894.

Abraham de Peyster

(*Above, right*) This statue was completed by George Bissell in 1896. De Peyster was an affluent gentleman who was born in 1657 in Nieu Amsterdam. He became a successful merchant and served, alternately, as mayor, alderman, chief justice, acting governor and colonel of militia. Since he was born at 3 Broadway, for many years this statue stood in Bowling Green. It was moved to Hanover Square in 1972. The pigeons on His Honor's head and shoulders are a more recent addition.

Originally Hanover Square was called Printing House Square. The first printing presses were set up here by William Bradford in 1693. He published various almanacs and pamphlets. But in 1725 he published the *New York Gazette*, the city's first newspaper. The presses were located at 81 Pearl Street and then moved to Park Row after a great fire in 1835.

Benjamin Franklin

This statue of Franklin the newspaperman was made by Ernst Plassmann in 1872. It stands at Printing House Square, where Nassau Street meets Park Row. His location is in front of where the *New York Times* was located. The *Times* occupied a five-story building built in 1859 and enlarged in 1888. In 1904 the paper moved uptown in its quest for additional space, to a newly-constructed skyscraper in Longacre Square, which was then renamed Times Square. The name Longacre prevailed for many years in a telephone exchange of the area and also as a Broadway Theatre. Horace Greeley, the editor of the *New York Tribune*, made the principal addresses at the dedication on January 12, 1872, as the statue was unveiled from its "star spangled robe" by an elderly statesman, inventor and artist—Samuel F.B. Morse.

Franklin holds a copy of his first newspaper, the *Pennsylvania Gazette.*

Printing House Square became so-named in the 1860s because of the concentration of nineteen newspapers in this area, chiefly the *New York Times*, the *Tribune*, the *Sun*, the *Telegram*, and the *New York Staats-Zeitung.* All chose to be close to the source of most of the news: City Hall.

George Washington

This statue, familiar to all Wall Streeters because of its prominent location in front of the former Subtreasury Building (now the Federal Hall National Memorial), was sculpted by John Quincy Adams Ward in 1883. It was sponsored by the New York State Chamber of Commerce for the centennial of George Washington's Inauguration in 1889. The statue shows the president lifting his hand from the Bible as he completes his swearing-in ceremony. The occasion was reenacted with great fanfare for the Bicentennial of Washington's Inauguration on April 30, 1989, including a prelude of a parade of tall ships in the harbor.

When Queen Elizabeth decided to visit New York in 1976, a respectful four days after July 4th, she addressed a large gathering on Wall Street from this same location. I was there, and it seemed that my colleague and I waited an eternity for her appearance, after we had seen her motorcade pass by Trinity Church. Apparently, she had to go around the building and enter through Pine Street because after all, my friend advised me, the Queen did not climb steps in public.

Integrity Protecting the Works of Man

The great pediment sculpture on the New York Stock Exchange was designed by John Quincy Adams Ward and executed by Paul Bartlett in 1903.

These larger than life-sized figures may be identified as follows: Integrity stands in the center, holding the world's business at her sides: mechanical arts, electricity, surveyors, and builders on the left, and mining and agriculture on the right—the products of invention versus those of the earth. The agriculture contingent includes a pregnant farmhand.

169

OUR LADY OF VICTORY

Wall Street Sculptures

(*Opposite*) Madonna and Child. This unusual Art Deco-styled Madonna and Child adorns the main entrance of Our Lady of Victory's church on Pine and William Streets. Located right in the very heart of Wall Street, Our Lady of Victory has heard many prayers over the years from bankers and brokers.

(*Above, left*) EZ Face. This is one of a series of large Easter Islanders that decorate the frieze on top of the EZ Directory Building at 80 Washington Street. Few people even know these sculptures exist on the hundred-year-old structure. But many people can readily identify the familiar red EZ Book of securities firms, which has been published semi-annually since 1927.

(*Above, right*) The Seamen's Bank. These friendly nautical motifs frame the main entrace of 72 Wall Street, which was designed for the Seamen's Bank for Savings by Benjamin Morris in 1926, one hundred years after the bank's founding. The same architect was also responsible for another nautically inspired building, the Cunard Line Building at 25 Broadway (1925), and also the Bank of New York Building at 48 Wall Street (1928). The Seamen's moved to 30 Wall Street in 1955 and this became a Williamsburg Savings Bank until its recent acquisition by the American International Group, Inc. This location also marks the original site of the New York Stock Exchange. On May 24, 1792, merchants and auctioneers gathered under a buttonwood tree and came to an agreement that led eventually to the formation of the Exchange in 1817.

American International Building

Seventy Pine Street was built by the Cities Service Company in 1932 and designed by Clinton & Russell. This 66-story building represents a wild celebration of Wall Street's riches. The company had its insignia duplicated throughout the lobby. (*Opposite*) On the outside, knowing the impact of the building could not be fully appreciated from street level (because of the proximity of other structures on the narrow streets), the company reproduced a model of the entire building.

(*Above, left*) The lobby of 70 Pine Street is one of the finest Art Deco experiences downtown. It has been faithfully restored and maintained by its new owner, American International Group, Inc. The building once contained the first double decker elevator cars ever installed in an office structure. They proved to be unpopular, however, and were soon replaced.

The building was once connected to 60 Wall Street via a bridge and was often referred to as the "60 Wall Tower."

Salomon Brothers & Hutzler, a somewhat sleepy bond house, was located at 60 Wall Street from 1922 to 1970, and Merrill Lynch, Pierce, Fenner & Bean was headquartered in the tower. Sixty Wall Street was torn down and the lot, remaining empty for many years, has now been graced with the new J.P. Morgan tower.

(*Above, right*) One of the lovely brass doors of American International Group's building at 72 Wall Street. This was originally built for the Seamen's Bank for Savings in 1926, which explains the maritime design. The Seamen's is the second oldest bank in New York after Bank of New York (whose headquarters at 48 Wall Street were designed by the same architect—Benjamin Morris). The original street address was 76 Wall Street, but seamen depositors persuaded management that the address be changed to 72 because the combination of 7 and 6 totalled 13, "a thing to make a good seaman worry."

The AIG Observatory

One of Wall Street's best-kept secrets is also one of its most spectacular: the rooftop observatory of Seventy Pine Street. Since its opening in 1932, the senior executives of first Cities Service, then Merrill Lynch and now American International Group have enjoyed this garden in the center of the financial district. The elevator pushes up through a trap door at the side of the observatory, behind the chrome gate at the right in the photograph, and then disappears completely upon its descent, leaving an unobstructed view in all directions. The brass globe attests to AIG's presence in international markets.

AIG is a leading international insurance and financial services organization and the largest underwriter of commercial and industrial insurance in the United States. With

more than 30,000 employees and assets of approximately $42 billion, its member companies write property, casualty, marine, life and financial services insurance in more than 130 countries.

The firm was started in China in 1919 as American Asiatic Underwriters by Cornelius Vander Starr. It soon established branches throughout the Far East, and during the 1940s-1960s expanded further into Latin America, Europe and the Middle East. Today, AIG is still growing in the Far East and is the largest foreign insurance organization in Japan. American International Group's world headquarters have been located in New York for fifty years.

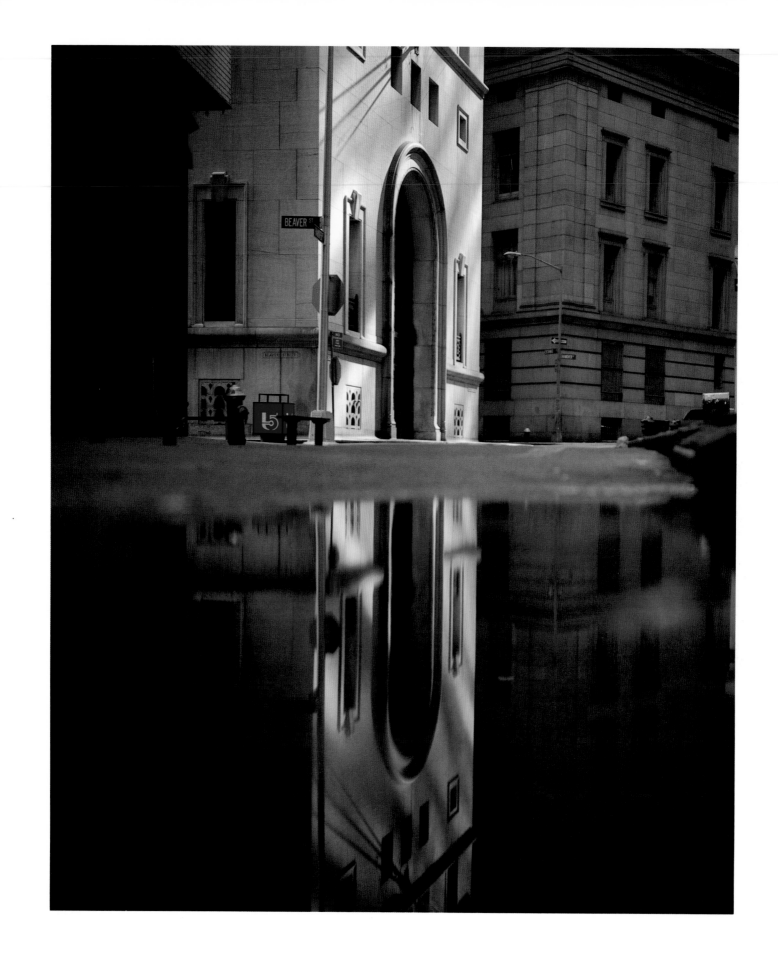

Early Morning

(*Opposite*) As the roosters crow, an early morning sun falls on the Farmers Trust Company. This is presently the entrance to the great 20 Exchange Place banking hall of Citibank. The National City Bank merged with the Farmers Loan & Trust Co. in 1929 and this structure became their main headquarters when it was completed in 1931.

This view is from Hanover Street which, along with Hanover Square, is named for the German family from which British monarchs were directly descended after 1714. Together with Nassau Street these are among the only streets whose names were not changed after the Revolutionary War. King and Queen Streets, for example, became Pine and Cedar.

Untitled

(*Above*) This is the name of the unnamed sculpture by Yu Yu Yang completed in 1973. This large intriguing sculpture is located at 88 Pine Street, also known as the Orient Overseas Building. It was commissioned by C.Y. Tung of the Orient Overseas Association.

The highly polished steel disk is twelve feet in diameter and weighs four thousand pounds. It appears to have been cut out of the matte-finished slab in front, set at a slight angle and reflecting the scene around it, including its own frame in this case. The disk and the hole create an interesting tension between each other. The latter might even be considered an oversized porthole, representing C.Y. Tung's shipping interests.

John Street Wreath

(*Above*) This is the front entrance to 127 John Street, built in 1969 by Emery Roth & Sons. The whimsical lobby and plaza, including a neon tunnel and other extravaganzas, were designed by Corchia-de Harak Associates, who were also responsible for the street-level pools and bridges of 77 Water Street. The developer of both properties was Mel Kaufman, who is the person to thank for these light touches on otherwise no-nonsense office buildings.

The End of the Road

(*Opposite*) Wall Street ends up at the East River near Old Slip and Gouverneur Lane. This has also been the end of the road for two large wire houses—Thomson McKinnon and Walston. Until recently, One Financial Square (in the left center of the photograph) was headquarters to Thomson McKinnon Securities, Inc. which is now being acquired by Prudential-Bache Securities, Inc. This building was designed by Edward Durell Stone Associates in 1987 and is located at the foot of Hanover Square on Front Street. Thomson McKinnon Securities, Inc., was founded in 1885

by Alexander W. Thomson, a grain merchant, and grew with acquisitions to become a retail brokerage firm with 154 branches and approximately two thousand registered representatives. During the 1970s it was known as Thomson, McKinnon, Auchincloss, Parker & Redpath.

To the right of One Financial Square is the former First Precinct office of the New York City Police Department which was designed as a rusticated Renaissance Revival palazzo—small in size but majestic in scale—by Hunt & Hunt in 1911.

At the left in the photograph is the edge of Seventy-seven Water Street, built in 1970 by Emery Roth & Sons. One of Wall Street's largest brokerage firms, which was so amok in the unautomated back office mess that even H. Ross Perot could not salvage it, was located here: Walston & Co. Walston tried to save two other famous firms, Glore, Forgan & Co. and Francis I. duPont. The group collapsed for the same reason that Goodbody was forced into the arms of Merrill Lynch in late 1970. None of them had adequately computerized their back offices and thus were unable to keep abreast of the increasing volume on the exchanges. They could not confirm trades either to their customers or deliveries of securities to or from other houses.

One Seaport Plaza

This gray granite building was designed by Swanke Haydon Connell & Partners and completed in 1983. Like many of its corporate neighbors, it is a large building of approximately one million square feet. It is headquarters to Prudential-Bache Securities and also Lloyds International Corporation. Outside a light rain falls on the evening limousines waiting to fulfill their uptown missions.

Inside, a collection of bright Frank Stellas enlivens a gray stone lobby. These oversized geometric designs can be seen from outside the building as well and glow in the puddle forming (appropriately) on Water Street.

Prudential-Bache Securities Inc.

Jules Bache and his family relocated to the United States from Germany in the 1870s. He took over a brokerage operation started by his uncle and named it J.S. Bache & Co. in 1882. His nephew Harold joined the firm in 1914 and renamed it Bache & Co. in 1945. For many decades the firm vied with Merrill Lynch as one of the largest securities brokerage firms in the country. During the early 1970s it made a series of strategic acquisitions, bringing it recognition in the areas of research and utility finance as well as additional brokerage capacity—Halsey, Stuart & Co., Shields & Co., and Model, Roland & Co. (which had the only foreign equities research department on Wall Street for many years).

In 1981 the firm was acquired by the Prudential Insurance Company of America and changed its name the fol-

lowing year to Prudential-Bache Securities Inc. Recently it acquired over one hundred and fifty offices and accounts from Thomson McKinnon Securities, Inc., a firm that had been founded in 1885. Today Prudential-Bache has almost four hundred offices in nineteen countries around the world. It employs approximately seventeen thousand, including over six thousand financial advisors. The firm offers a wide range of products, from securities and banking services to retirement planning, financing packages for municipalities, and corporate reorganization advice and financing. Its ties to the Prudential provide a strong source of capital for its many private transactions. In addition, the firm has developed industry leadership in the offering and management of closed-end investment companies.

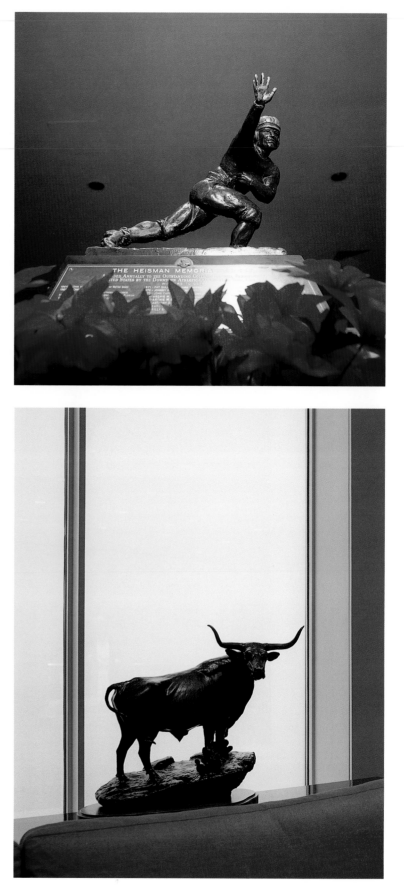

Famous Wall Street Bronzes

A sampling of famous Wall Street bronzes: (*above*) the Heisman Trophy at the Downtown Athletic Club, college football's most coveted award and named for a famous football coach of the 1930-1950s, John Heisman; (*right*) Merrill Lynch's famous bull, which became the firm's mascot when it switched its advertising focus from "We the People"; (*opposite, top*) Telerate's Rodins, easily the largest such collection in the financial district if not in New York; and (*opposite, bottom*) the New York Stock Exchange's familiar bull and bear duo.

WALL STREET WEST

Ninety West Street

This lovely limestone and terra cotta building was completed in 1907 and designed by Cass Gilbert, who gave us the Custom House in 1907 and the Woolworth Building in 1913. Until its upper-floor colonnades and copper mansard roof were illuminated in 1985, few people were aware of the extraordinary beauty of this out-of-the-way building.

The photograph at the left shows a marked contrast of three generations of architecture: the flamboyance of Beaux Arts, the plain International School design of One Bankers Trust Plaza in the foreground (1974) (whose mezzanine plaza rings the subjects in the photograph), and the more fanciful design of Cesar Pelli's Oppenheimer & Company Tower at the World Financial Center (1985).

Sphere for Plaza Fountain

(*Above*) The bronze globe is by Fritz Koenig, who completed it in 1971. The ruptured sphere suggests both cosmic forces as well as cellular life. It was commissioned by the Port Authority of New York & New Jersey as part of its art-in-architecture program. The Authority also commissioned works by Alexander Calder and Louise Nevelson.

The Plaza of the World Trade Center

(*Opposite*) The graceful arches of Tower Number One, with Christmas trees grouped along the edge, are reflected on the plaza's wet pavement during a winter drizzle. For a brief moment the viewer is reminded of the Metropolitan Opera House at Lincoln Center. This is the only gentle aspect of the twin towers whose relentless soar is difficult to grasp comfortably even after almost twenty years. The plaza, with its 25-foot bronze sphere by Fritz Koenig in the center, is often devoid of people—certainly when compared with the flow of pedestrians through the underground concourse. It does, however, offer a secret escape on sunny days to enjoy a moment of relative solitude.

The World Trade Center consists of seven office buildings, six of which were designed by Minoru Yamaski and Emery Roth & Sons. They were completed as follows: 2 W.T.C. (1972); 1 W.T.C. (1973); 5 W.T.C. (1972); 4 W.T.C. (1977); and 6 W.T.C. (1974). No. Seven was built in 1987 by Emery Roth & Sons. The aggregate amount of office space exceeds ten million square feet —over seven times that of the Empire State Building.

The Vista Hotel

(*Above, left*) Shown at the left in the photograph, this hotel joined the twin towers at the World Trade Center in 1981, nine years after the first tower was constructed. Skidmore, Owings & Merrill have provided a handsome design of horizontal aluminum and glass stripes on a soft, bow front structure. The Vista Hotel provides a refreshing complement to the stark twin towers.

St. Nicholas Church

(*Above, right*) Resting at the feet of the twin towers is the little St. Nicholas Church (1832), a Hellenic Orthodox church on Cedar Street. This is one of the last vestiges of the days when lower Washington Street was a neighborhood of Greeks, Lebanese, Syrians, and Armenians.

The twin towers rise to an extraordinary height of 110 stories, more than a quarter of a mile above street level. When the World Trade Center was under construction in 1967, a cannon was discovered during excavation, marked with the insignia of the Dutch West India Company. It probably belonged to Captain Adriaen Block's *Tiger* which burned at this location in 1613, forcing Block and his crew to be the first European residents on Manhattan that winter.

Contrasting Spires

(*Opposite*) New York is a city of contrasts and none is greater than the view of the twin towers from the churchyard of St. Paul's Chapel. The World Trade Center project was commissioned by the Port Authority of New York & New Jersey, which decided to squeeze maximum space out of it. The results are oversized, flat topped boxes that are a bit too harsh, even today, for a neighborhood that otherwise consists largely of a cluster of filigreed towers. The disheveled neighborhood of electronics stores called Radio Row that was replaced by the World Trade Center is now only a memory to some.

In their design of the twin towers, the architects did accomplish an interesting engineering feat: the walls are load-bearing, which is unusual in this era of steel frame construction. The walls are like a mesh cage supporting the entire building.

Dean Witter Reynolds Inc.

Dean, Jean and Guy Witter formed this firm in San Francisco in 1924, primarily as a dealer in municipal and corporate debt obligations. It was a new firm, although Dean Witter had formed an earlier partnership in April 1914 with Charles Blyth to conduct a general brokerage and investment banking business, also out of San Francisco. In 1929, Dean Witter opened an office in New York (although it was not until almost sixty years later that New York and not San Francisco was considered the firm's principal headquarters). Also in 1929 it became a member firm of the New York Stock Exchange for the first time. Given the importance of attracting qualified sales representatives, Dean Witter & Co. established one of the first for-

mal brokers' training programs in 1945. The photograph above shows today's training center—the only one of the major firms that is maintained in the Wall Street area.

Dean Witter & Co. Incorporated sold its shares to the public in 1972, acquired Laird, Bissel & Meads in 1973 and Reynolds & Co. in 1978. Through these acquisitions and internal growth, Dean Witter became the first brokerage house with offices in all fifty states and the District of Columbia in 1979. Additional acquisitions were also made in the insurance field (Surety Life in 1976 and Benefit Life in 1981.) In December 1981, Dean Witter joined Sears Roebuck & Co. as the nucleus of its financial services group.

American Express Company

The firm is located at Three World Financial Center, which was completed in 1985, designed by Cesar Pelli, Dean of the Yale School of Architecture, and Adamson Associates.

From its tasteful entrance and spectacular lobby the viewer can see that American Express is an exceptional firm. It conducts its affairs the way it furnishes its facilities —just a cut above the rest. This is where one would expect the issuer of the original "gold" charge card and the originator of the international travelers' checks to be headquartered. The strong black marble columns and the dramatic geometry of the ivory, black and rust floor are reminiscent of the great banking halls of the 1920s.

It is fortunate that American Express has chosen to remain a prominent fixture in the Wall Street community since its inception. It is a full financial service organization in the broadest sense, with brokerage, overseas banking, insurance, travel and charge card activities—a greater spectrum than any other organization. Many banks and securities firms may be larger both in assets and employees, and some of these also may offer credit card services, but none do so with the élan of American Express.

The American Express Company was organized on March 18, 1850 to carry on the business originally established nine years earlier by Henry Wells to transport goods, valuables, and bank remittances between New York City and various cities upstate. By 1852 Henry Wells and the company secretary, William Fargo, decided to expand their services west of Missouri, which was as far as the railroad had extended. They formed a separate company to do so. American Express concentrated on delivery of valuable shipments via the railroad and assisted the U.S. Government with the delivery of supplies to army depots during the Civil War.

In 1891 the company introduced the Travelers Cheque to replace the cumbersome letter of credit that was often used by overseas travelers. Within ten years the company was issuing over $6 million travelers' checks annually. Today sales are in the billions of dollars in a variety of international currencies.

By 1915 American Express had expanded into another important area: travel, which during the 1920s and again beginning in the 1950s has become an increasingly important part of the firm's activities.

With the prosperity of the 1950s, and the increase in travel and entertainment, American Express recognized another opportunity: a charge card. During the first year of its introduction in 1958, the company issued 253,000 cards. It also played a major role in persuading the Civil Aviation Board to allow airline ticket purchases with charge cards. The first cards were paperboard, but by the following year the familiar plastic card was in full bloom. Railroads, cruise lines, hotels, and oil companies all began accepting the card during the early 1960s, which by then was also becoming available in foreign currencies includ-

ing Venezuelan bolivars and Yugoslav dinars. In 1972 Macy's became the first major department store to accept the card. Today there are over 30 million green, gold and platinum cards in force, being accepted at approximately 2.3 million service establishments worldwide—a truly remarkable accomplishment for an institution that, unlike its commercial banking competitors, had no pre-exisiting customer base to draw from.

American Express has also expanded into the fields of investment banking, asset management and insurance. The firm's initial venture into the securities business was its 1966 acquisition of W.H. Morton & Co., an underwriter and distributor of corporate and government bonds. In 1981 it acquired Shearson Loeb Rhoades, Inc., the second largest securities firm in the country, which subsequently acquired Lehman Brothers, Kuhn, Loeb & Co. Inc. and the E.F. Hutton Group, Inc.

American Express Company

(*Opposite, top*) The board room in the American Express Tower has a table as large as the New York Stock Exchange's board room.

(*Opposite, bottom*) The Board of Directors' main dining room is capable of serving up to ninety guests. At dinner this evening entertainment is being provided by the Woolworth Building.

(*Above*) The visitor's library has a collection of rare old books, globes, telescopes, and other antiques appropriate for a firm that has had a strong international presence for over one hundred years. The balcony is planted with dwarf pine trees and other vegetation that one imagines seeing from an English manor house and not on the top floor of the American Express Tower.

Shearson Lehman Hutton Inc.

Shearson Lehman Brothers Inc.   E.F. Hutton & Co., Inc.

Shearson Lehman/American Express

Shearson/American Express   Lehman Brothers Kuhn Loeb & Co., Inc.

Foster & Marshall
Robinson-Humphrey & Co.
Davis, Skaggs & Co.

Shearson Loeb Rhoades

Lehman Brothers
Abraham & Co.

Kuhn, Loeb & Co.

Shearson Hayden Stone   Loeb Rhoades Hornblower & Co.

Faulkner, Dawkins & Sullivan
Reinholdt & Gardner
Lamson Brothers & Co.

Shearson
Hammill & Co.

Hentz & Co.

Hayden Stone
& Co.

CBWL
Hayden Stone

Loeb Rhoades & Co.   Hornblower Weeks, Noyes & Trask

Edwards & Hanley

Carl M. Loeb   Rhoades & Co.

Hayden Stone & Co.
Charles Westheimer & Co.
Lee Higginson Corp.

Cogan, Berlind, Weil & Levitt

Carter, Berlind
& Weill

Bernstein-
Macaulay

Carter, Berlind, Potoma & Weill

Hornblower & Weeks
Hemphill Noyes & Co.

Spencer Trask & Co.

Hornblower & Weeks   Hemphill Noyes & Co.

Shearson Lehman Hutton Inc.

This is clearly one of the most successful establishments on Wall Street today, with a legacy that reads like a *Who's Who* of corporate finance. The firm recently reported profits of $96 million on revenues of over $10 billion. It has approximately $100 billion under various asset management programs, handled 229 merger and acquisition transactions in 1988 and was lead or co-lead manager in over six hundred public underwritings aggregating approximately $56 billion.

The history of Shearson Lehman Hutton Inc. is best described in the family tree *(opposite)*. It probably contains a greater number of famous Wall Street houses than all other firms combined. Two of Wall Street's oldest and most prominent investment banking partnerships were Kuhn, Loeb & Co. (1867) and Lehman Brothers (1850). During the latter part of the nineteenth century and well into the present one, Kuhn Loeb was highly regarded as a powerful house ranking at or near the top of most lists, along with J.P. Morgan & Co. It played a major role in financing the American transportation industries and was active in overseas capital markets by the turn of the century —all from a single office in New York run by a handful of partners.

Lehman Brothers' origins date from 1850 when it was engaged primarily in trading cotton and other merchandise. In fact, it helped organize the New York Cotton Exchange in 1870, which was the first experiment in commodity futures trading. Hedging transactions brought a stability to the industry for the benefit of growers, consumers and manufacturers. In 1906 Lehman Brothers co-managed an offering for Sears, Roebuck & Co., beginning a long tradition of assistance in the financing of retailers and consumer goods manufacturers.

With respect to research, Spencer Trask & Co. was the jewel acquisition that came to the firm via Hornblower & Weeks, Hemphill, Noyes & Co. in 1979. This firm established the first securities research department on Wall Street in 1894—to meet the increasing demand for current information on industrial and utility companies.

The department's head, John Moody, was motivated by its success to leave the firm and form Moody's Manual, the predecessor of Moody's Investors Service. Another interesting note about Spencer Trask is that it became one of the first firms to have electric lights, and it pioneered in interbranch communications, linking them in 1881 with a private wire system. Spencer Trask was Thomas Edison's principal financial backer. Shearson Lehman Hutton's interest in research and communications continues in full force today. In 1986, it opened a twenty-four-hour information services facility, designed to collect and process data from offices around the world and named for the firm's former Vice Chairman, Dwight Faulkner.

The Winter Garden at the World Financial Center

This is a welcome, sunny structure similar in spirit if not design to London's Crystal Palace of the last century. Its palm-filled interior is roughly the size of Grand Central's concourse and is easily one of the greatest interior spaces constructed during the twentieth century. The forty-foot trees barely reach halfway to the top. There are only sixteen trees, not a forest, so they become part of the architecture.

During the evenings and weekends Olympia & York, in cooperation with American Express Company and Merrill Lynch & Company, sponsor a wide variety of cultural events ranging from the Brooklyn Philharmonic, ballroom dancing and the Vienna Boys' Choir to Bali dancing and the Herbie Hancock Trio.

Cesar Pelli and his wife designed the Winter Palace in 1988 as a living room for the twenty thousand workers in the World Financial Center—a place to be in instead of simply to pass through.

Outside the Winter Garden

The landscape architect was Paul Friedberg & Partners which was also responsible for the redesign of Bowling Green and Jeannette Plaza. Although the Winter Garden appears dwarfed by its surrounding neighbors, the enormous height of this great space may be grasped by noticing the tops of the palm trees in the lower part of the photograph. The trees are already forty feet tall. A cluster of Christmas trees rings the outside plaza, duplicating similar clusters inside.

The Oppenheimer Tower and Dow Jones Building

This is One World Financial Center (1985). At the left in
the photograph is Cass Gilbert's Ninety West Street (1907).
These structures are seventy-eight years apart and yet they
are totally compatible today.

The World Financial Center

Shown here are Merrill Lynch & Co.'s world headquarters, No. 4 World Financial Center (1985) (*above*), and American Express Company headquarters, No. 3 World Financial Center (1986) (*opposite*). Cesar Pelli was the design architect for both towers, assisted by Haines Lundberg Waehler on Merrill Lynch's and by Adamson Associates on American Express's.

All four towers at the World Financial Center are of different heights and are topped by different roofs. Merrill Lynch has a stepped pyramid on its North Tower

(shown here) and a dome on its South Tower. American Express has a regular pyramid and Oppenheimer & Co. has a mastaba (a flat-topped pyramid). The entire World Financial Center complex contains over seven million square feet of space. It consists of four towers and two gatehouses, all of glass and granite, and all set slightly irregularly to each other in order to soften the harsh impact of the oversized twin towers of the neighboring World Trade Center.

In the foreground is the new North Cove being devel-

oped by Watermark Associates and designed to return New York to an era of mega-yachting not seen since 1929. At the turn of the century, the New York Yacht Club's fleet included 195 sailboats and 207 steamships, the largest of which was the *Lysistrata* belonging to the *New York Herald* publisher James Gordon Bennett. It was a 314-foot, 2,282-ton steamer that required a full-time crew of a hundred.

City of the world! (for all races are here,
All the lands of the earth make contributions here;)

City of the sea! city of hurried and glittering tides!
City whose gleeful tides
*   continually rush or recede,*
*   whirling in and out with eddies and foam!*
City of wharves and stores—city of tall facades of
*   marble and iron!*
Proud and passionate city—meddlesome, mad,
*   extravagant city!*

Walt Whitman
Leaves of Grass (1881)

Christmas at Merrill Lynch & Co.

These are some of the many decorations at the firm's world headquarters, to which it moved from One Liberty Plaza in early 1987. This enormous firm occupies two of the four towers at the World Financial Center.

The Merrill Lynch & Co. name was adopted on October 15, 1915 as a successor to the firm started by Charles E. Merrill in 1914. Edmund Lynch joined later that year. Messrs. Merrill and Lynch felt there were many potential investors outside the social and economic elite catered to by the old-line Wall Street houses. They also pioneered in raising capital for the emerging chain store industry such as Kresge's and McCrory's. In fact the McCrory offering had to be sold twice because the outbreak of war in Europe in 1914 caused the New York Stock Exchange to close for *four months* during the middle of the firm's offering. It was subsequently reoffered the following year.

The firm hired Wall Street's first bond saleswoman in 1919, Annie Grimes, opened its uptown New York office

every weekday evening from 7 p.m. to 9 p.m. beginning in 1924, in order to cater to the "average investor," and continued to concentrate on raising capital for the retail chains. In 1930, Merrill Lynch transferred most of its business to E.A. Pierce & Co., founded in 1885 and by then the nation's largest wire house. During the 1920s, Pierce had established branches across the country, connected by a network of private wires to transmit orders and quotations. In 1940 Charles Merrill was persuaded to combine Merrill Lynch with Pierce to create a new style of brokerage company intent on "bringing Wall Street to Main Street."

In 1941 Merrill Lynch was the first Wall Street firm to issue an annual report showing its operating results for the year. Also in that year it merged with Fenner & Beane which resulted in offices in ninety-two cities around the country. In 1956 the firm was selected as one of seven managers of the initial public offering for Ford Motor

Company, giving Merrill Lynch its first billion-dollar underwriting year. In 1955 the firm became one of the first American businesses to computerize its operations with the purchase of three IBM 650s, and it was the first Wall Street firm to install the more powerful, second generation, transistorized IBM 7080. During the late 1960s the surge in trading volume in the New York Stock Exchange caught many firms unprepared for the commensurate paperwork. Trade confirmations and securities certificates were lost, and by the second half of 1970, many major firms were on the verge of collapse or had already gone under. In October 1970, the fifth largest member firm was about to fail. Had it done so, the Exchange would have had a serious panic and therefore Merrill Lynch was asked to step in to absorb the floundering Goodbody & Co. Merrill Lynch was the only firm capable of handling such an acquisition. By 1971 it had digested the assignment and was ready to sell its shares to the public for the first time. It was the second Exchange member to do so after Donaldson, Lufkin & Jenrette. In April 1978 the firm acquired the prestigious, old-line investment banking house of White, Weld & Co.

In 1977 Merrill Lynch created the Cash Management Account, the world's first combined money market/ brokerage/credit card account. Currently CMA has over $190 billion under management. Today Merrill Lynch has approximately 12,300 registered representatives in over 450 offices throughout the world. Its equity capital is approximately $3.5 billion making it the largest and clearly one of the most successful investment banking and securities firms in the country, based on the primary objective of serving the investment and financial needs of individuals and institutions.

Merrill Lynch & Co.

The interiors of Merrill Lynch are finished with the refinement and detail that have been absent from new office structures for the past thirty years. The executive floors are indicative of the distance Merrill Lynch has come in the same time span from being simply a large wire house, distributing other firms' offerings, to being the largest player in the field of investment banking.

In one of the most successful Wall Street mergers of the past decade, Merrill Lynch acquired White, Weld & Co. in 1978. This was an old-line firm with innovative financing techniques, an international presence, and a greater string of initial public stock offerings during the 1960s and 1970s than any other firm. At one point in 1969 White, Weld & Co. had more deals in registration with the Securities & Exchange Commission (thirty-two) than it had professionals in its corporate finance department (thirty-one). There were fifty-three initial public of-

ferings and secondary distributions that year. The firm was a pioneer in the use of warrants and unit offerings of notes and equity in order to help its pipeline utility clients raise the large amounts of capital needed to construct natural gas transmission facilities across the country in the 1950s and 1960s. It was early to recognize the growth of the electronics businesses, and both Wang Laboratories and Control Data became major clients, among others. White Weld was also known for its expertise in broadcasting and cable television, as well as venture capital (it helped launch Federal Express). Offshore it pioneered in the creation and use of Eurobonds when the Interest Equalization Tax went into effect in 1965. During the next ten years it underwrote and made markets in more international debt instruments than any other firm on either side of the Atlantic.

Merrill's Trading Floors

Merrill Lynch & Co. has three trading floors at the World Financial Center, each two stories in height, for an aggregate of approximately 80,000 square feet of floor space.

On the fixed-income floor, shown above, there are 600 desks. It is the largest private trading room in the world.

All three trading floors contain an aggregate of 1200 desks.

In 1988 Merrill Lynch processed an average of 80,000 trades a day for its 7.5 million customers. On a typical trading day its equity transactions account for almost one quarter of the New York Stock Exchange volume.

The Wall Street Journal

(*Above, left*) Dow Jones & Co.'s *Wall Street Journal* originates from the company's building at the World Financial Center. The view above is of the *Journal's* news desk.

(*Below, left*) An artist is creating a Christmas drawing utilizing the pinpoint design that has become a tradition with the newspaper. Photographs are rarely used. They are converted into engraving-like drawings, as may be seen on the artist's table, with each such conversion taking four to six hours.

This is the headquarters for the famous publishing firm organized in 1882 by Charles Henry Dow and Edward Jones. Their first financial newsletter was called the *Customers' Afternoon Letter* which evolved into *The Wall Street Journal* by 1889. By 1884 they had started another important element of American financial information—the Dow Jones Average, consisting of eleven stocks listed on the New York Stock Exchange. *Barron's National Business and Financial Weekly* was started in 1921 with Clarence Barron as its first editor. The tabloid was an immediate success and reached a circulation of 30,000 in its sixth year.

The architect of today's *Journal* was Bernard Kilgore who became managing editor in 1941. He turned the financial newspaper into one that encompassed all aspects of business, economics and consumer affairs as well as everything else that had an impact on business.

The *Journal* was able to become a national newspaper before the advent of microwave and space satellite transmission (which are used today) with an invention by one of its employees, Joseph Ackell. He repaired the paper's news tickers and came up with a method of inputting data onto perforated tape much like a player piano. The tape was played by typesetting machines around the country with the stories having to be manually typeset only once.

Today, thanks in part to more advanced transmission technology, *The Wall Street Journal* has a paid circulation of approximately two million and is the largest newspaper in the United States.

Battery Park City

(*Opposite*) New residential buildings along Rector Place, at the southern edge of the World Financial Center, demonstrate a variety of styles by different architects in a harmonizing, non-competing group. The totality of the complex was the objective, the means were left up to the individual firms in order to provide a mixture of styles.

The twin residential towers of Liberty House and Liberty Terrace frame the towers of the World Trade Center and the Oppenheimer Tower. The apartments in the foreground are called Rector Place.

(*Above*) A rich variety of apartments and office structures may be seen from South Cove. From the left are: the Regatta, the Merrill Lynch South Tower, the Oppenheimer Tower, the World Trade Center Towers, the new Rector Place Apartment Tower, One Bankers Trust Plaza, and One Liberty Plaza.

Wall Street from South Cove

(*Above*) This is the view from the rocks of South Cove. It is hard to imagine that the world's largest financial district is only a few yards away from this rugged shoreline. Battery Park City and the World Financial Center are part of an extraordinary 92-acre landfill extending from Battery Park itself up to Chambers Street. It is a gift from the World Trade Center whose excavation of over one million cubic yards of soil was deposited here. From the left in the pho-

tograph are: One Bankers Trust Plaza, One Liberty Plaza, 19 Rector Street, the Chase Manhattan Bank, the Irving Trust Company Tower, 67 Broadway, 40 Wall Street's pyramid, two new buildings at 47 and 45 Broadway, the Bank of New York's West Street offices, the Downtown Athletic Club and 17 Battery Place.

Governor Nelson Rockefeller first proposed creating a Battery Park City in the 1960s; the state owns the land.

After several false starts at design, many of which conceived of the City as separate from the rest of its urban environment, a master plan was presented by Cooper, Eckstut Associates that saw the entire project as an historical extension of the city's best waterfront communities rather than in futuristic isolation. The streets are aligned with the city's grid; the esplanade with its turn-of-the-century lamps is more old-fashioned than Carl Schurz Park; the canopied apartment foyers and townhouses on South End Avenue and vicinity might just as well have come from East End Avenue.

Stanton Eckstut was responsible for the southern residential areas, which are designed to reflect the neighborhoods of Gramercy Park, Riverside Drive, and Tudor City. The result is an entirely new neighborhood with a distinctive, historical patina.

Christmas in Rector Park

The park is located at the intersection of South End Avenue and Rector Place. Innocenti & Webel with Vollmer Associates were the landscape architects who designed a finely detailed space in keeping with the spirit of Gramercy Park. In this case, however, there are open sections in the fence so a key is not needed. The buildings on the left are Battery Pointe and Liberty Terrace, 300 and 380 Rector Place, respectively, and on the right is River Rose at 333 Rector Place.

An Evening Stroll on the Esplanade

This extraordinary gift to the city extends for over a mile at the edge of Battery Park City. It was designed by Stanton Eckstut and built from 1983 to 1989. He has incorporated some of the best of New York's existing parks, including the promenades at Carl Schurz Park and Brooklyn Heights. The benches are replicas of the turn-of-the-century cast-iron and wood design that were popular many years ago, as were the Victorian lampposts that have also been carefully duplicated.

Eventually the Esplanade will connect with Battery Park itself, and, upon completion of the northern section of Battery Park City, it will be nearly two miles long. Accessible to all and frequented by few, it is an excellent place for a quiet walk in the early evening, where the soothing clang of a buoy is the only sound one hears.

Harrison Street

(*Opposite*) Just north of the World Financial Center is a cluster of ten row houses on Harrison Street. They are all of the Federal period and date from 1819 to 1928. Two were designed by John McComb, who designed City Hall. They represent a fine example of the houses that became popular at the time—three-story brick facades, three bays across, with double dormers. They were generally built in units of three, with common walls.

The row house evolved because the city adopted a plan in 1811 to organize its future development according to a grid system of twelve avenues and perpendicular streets. Federal row houses were built along the grid, including the residential development of the estate of a classical scholar, Clement Clarke Moore. His estate was named Chelsea and was developed between Eighth Avenue and the Hudson River, from 20th to 28th Streets.

Moore is better known for his Christmas poem, "A Visit from St. Nicholas."

Washington Market Park

(*Above*) A memorial to the famous outdoor Washington Market, this little jewel on Greenwich Street between Chambers and Duane Streets is a modern interpretation of the best of Olmstead and Vaux: hills, a gazebo, a witty fence, and even some Art Deco ornaments from the old West Side Highway.

Washington Market sprang up on the West Side when shipping shifted from the South Street area over to the Hudson or North River after the Civil War. The Hudson was able to accommodate the larger and more numerous steam-powered vessels. Increased trucking and congestion resulted in the construction of the West Side (Miller) Highway, which lasted until the early 1980s. The Washington Market Park contains two stone Art Deco entrance monuments from the elevated highway, each with an automobile headlight in its leading edge.

Smith Barney, Harris Upham, Inc.

In 1969, Smith, Barney & Co. became the first of the old-line issuing houses to move uptown, from its headquarters of many years at 20 Broad Street. It chose a site on Avenue of the Americas, then in the throes of developing as a new business center in New York, for its convenience to clients and to avoid the Wall Street area's congestion. The uptown area subsequently became "Wall Street North," attracting Morgan Stanley, Blyth, Eastman Dillon & Co. and Paine, Webber, Jackson & Curtis, among others.

The firm's antecedents are Chas. D. Barney & Co. founded in Philadelphia in 1873 by a son-in-law of the famed nineteenth-century financier Jay Cooke, and Edward B. Smith & Co., also founded in Philadelphia, in 1892. Both firms were investment banking and brokerage houses for the carriage trade. The two merged in 1937 to form Smith, Barney & Co.

Although the firm had regional offices in the principal cities in the United States and overseas, it was not until its acquisition of Harris, Upham & Co. in 1976 that it had a substantial retail distribution capacity. Today, Smith Barney, Harris Upham & Co. has more than 100 offices in the U.S. and overseas, and some 2,500 brokers. Its particular strengths are municipal bond underwriting and trading, corporate finance, institutional and individual investor brokerage services, and securities research. Its research department has continuously distinguished itself in national rankings.

Shown in the photographs above are Alan Shaw's unique chart room, the largest on Wall Street (with records going back to the 1880s), and a view of the firm's main reception area showing a portrait of Chas. Barney.

Smith Barney's Fountain

This section of Sixth Avenue contains three of the industry's most prominent firms—Smith Barney, Morgan Stanley and Paine Webber, all of whom have relocated here in the past twenty years.

WALL STREET NORTH

Morgan Stanley & Co.

(*Above*) The equity trading desk of Morgan Stanley, and (*opposite*) two of the firm's founding partners, Henry S. Morgan and Harold Stanley.

This firm was organized on September 16, 1935 principally by four partners of J.P. Morgan & Company, who chose to remain in investment banking, and two from Drexel & Co. There were nine partners in all and a total capital of $7 million. Its initial offices were located at Two Wall Street, where it remained for almost forty years. Its capital was deemed sufficient well into the 1960s and it chose to be a conspicuously small though eminently prestigious organization. Its total employment was about 100, with the partners sharing an open room with rolltop desks and the staff grouped in modest quarters many of which had linoleum floors.

From the beginning Morgan Stanley sought the managership of security issues, rather than participations in underwriting syndicates. It remained a wholesale organization for many years, underwriting and selling to dealers. In the first thirty-two years of its existence it had only one office. Then in 1967 it opened an office in Paris, Morgan & Cie. International, in a joint venture with Morgan Guaranty Trust Company. Also in 1967 it relocated its headquarters from Two Wall Street to 140 Broadway. The pace of change has been more rapid in recent years at Morgan Stanley. The turning point was a 1971 planning meeting that brought the recognition that the firm would have to grow, distribute, build an equity trading and research department, and add to its back office. The firm relocated to midtown in 1973, started to build a research department that year, and sold its shares to the public in 1986. None of these were first steps, but these were viewed in the industry as significant.

For the first four decades the firm's employment was approximately 100 people. It presently employs over 6,400 and only 22 percent of its revenues derive from investment banking.

When Judge Harold Medina wrote about the seventeen leading investment banking houses in 1953, he started with Morgan Stanley. The same would be true today. It is a unique firm that has managed to do first-class business in a first-class way no matter which way the winds are blowing.

PaineWebber Incorporated

In July 1879 Charles Cabot Jackson and Laurence Curtis opened a brokerage office on Congress Street in Boston. One year later, William A. Paine and Wallace C. Webber opened their office up the street. When these two firms merged in 1942 to form Paine, Webber, Jackson & Curtis, they had grown to a combined total of 23 branch offices.

In 1963, the firm moved its headquarters to New York, was incorporated in 1970, and went public in 1972 with the acquisition of Abacus Fund, Inc., a listed, closed-end investment company. Through the acquisitions of Abbott, Proctor & Paine in 1970; F.S. Smithers & Co. and Mitchum, Jones & Templeton Inc. in 1973; and Rotan Mosle Financial Corp. in 1983, Paine Webber, Jackson & Curtis built a strong, nationwide distribution network.

In 1977, it acquired Mitchell Hutchins, Inc., a firm that traced its history to 1919 and had evolved to become one of America's leading equity research boutiques.

Two years later, Blyth, Eastman Dillon & Co. was acquired, adding seventy branch offices and more than seven hundred investment executives in addition to a well-developed investment banking capability.

Blyth, too, had a long and involved Wall Street history. The original firm was founded in San Francisco in 1914 by Charles Blyth and Dean Witter. It was known as Blyth, Witter & Co. until 1928 when Dean Witter left to set up his own brokerage business. In 1935, Charles Mitchell, former chairman of the National City Bank of New York and a director of the Federal Reserve Bank of New York,

joined the firm to assist in developing its underwriting and distribution businesses which were intended to complement the company's established West Coast investment banking operation. Blyth & Co. merged with Eastman Dillon Union Securities & Co. in 1972. Eastman Dillon was a full-line investment banking firm, founded in Pennsylvania in 1912 by Herbert Dillon and Thomas Eastman, which merged with Union Securities in 1956. Union Securities had been founded in 1939 to assume the underwriting business of J.&W. Seligman and established a successful track record during the 1940s and 1950s in what is known today as merchant banking: buying up, restructuring, and selling companies.

In 1985 the firm moved its headquarters from 140 Broadway, to 1285 Avenue of the Americas in midtown, and the following year a new complex at Lincoln Harbor in New Jersey became home to the firm's technology and transaction processing operations.

Today, Paine Webber is a full-service securities firm serving the investment and capital needs of a worldwide client base. Its principal lines of business include retail brokerage, investment and merchant banking, trading and asset management, each supported by a distinguished research capability and state-of-the-art technology support systems. With nearly 13,000 employees (including 4,500 registered investment executives) in 190 offices worldwide and a capital base of $1.4 billion, it remains one of the few independent, publicly held firms in its industry.

The First Boston Corporation

This firm came into existence as the result of the impact of the Glass-Steagall Act on the securities affiliates of two great banking institutions: the First National Bank of Boston and the Chase National Bank. It is thus the successor to the First of Boston Corporation and Chase Harris Forbes Corporation. The latter started in Chicago in 1882 and its Chicago business was transferred to Harris Trust & Savings Bank in 1907. The New York and Boston offices were acquired by Chase Securities Corporation in 1930.

The securities affiliate of First National Bank of Boston became a publicly held corporation on June 15, 1934. First of Boston Corporation became an independent entity and is thus the oldest publicly-held major investment banking firm. It acquired the assets and goodwill of Chase Harris Forbes in 1934 and on July 31, 1946, Mellon Securities Corporation was merged into the First Boston Corporation.

During the 1940s and 1950s, First Boston excelled at large, complex industrial financings: initial debt offerings for the World Bank, Hydro Quebec, and a 2.2 million share offering for Gulf Oil Corporation in 1948 (the largest equity offering until that time). In 1959 it reintroduced the credit of Japan to the American markets with the first offerings by the government since 1930.

Because it was publicly-owned, First Boston was not allowed to join the New York Stock Exchange and therefore built up its reputation as an aggressive dealer in the "third market." This consisted of listed securities traded over-the-counter. The firm subsequently joined the Stock Exchange in 1971 when another firm, Donaldson, Lufkin

& Jenrette, forced the public ownership issue. In fact, when the latter firm decided to be the second securities firm to go public in 1970 it turned to First Boston to manage the issue. The firm became the securities industry's investment banker, managing or advising in the initial public offerings for Reynolds Securities Inc., Merrill Lynch, and Paine Webber.

In 1978 First Boston entered into a global partnership with Financière Credit Suisse – First Boston (CSFB), through a cross-sharing agreement. This new partnership became the unquestioned leader in the Euro-capital markets. In 1982 First Boston managed the first adjustable rate preferred stock ("ARP") issue and the next year developed the Collateralized Mortgage Obligation ("CMO") followed by other asset-backed securities. It became the leading agent

for brokered master notes (a commercial paper substitute) and in 1981 moved to new headquarters at Park Avenue Plaza, a facility it helped to finance which was made possible through one of the largest purchases and transfers of air-rights at the time.

First Boston had 1889 employees in 1982 and by 1987 it had grown to over 5,000, an annual growth rate of 24%. The growth rate has now abated, and the firm is concentrating on solidifying its client relationships. In what is often perceived to be a transaction-driven business, First Boston believes that its strong advisory capability coupled with first-rate transaction implementation is essential. This is true whether the financing is straightforward or complex; whether it is a restructuring, long term project or simply giving advice on worldwide transactions.

First Boston's trading floor

(*Above*) Today, First Boston directs its securities activities
from a 40,000 square-foot trading floor that at the time
of its construction was the largest private trading room
in the world. With offices throughout the world, the firm
is able to maintain round-the-clock trading in several thousands of securities in a variety of currencies.

On December 22, 1988 in conjunction with the combination of the firm's parent company, First Boston, Inc.,
and Financière Credit Suisse-First Boston, the combined
entity became a privately-held company and was renamed
CS First Boston, Inc.

Bear, Stearns & Co. Inc.

(*Opposite*) This is the atrium of Bear Stearns with its double spiral staircases connecting three floors at its new midtown headquarters. The firm was founded as a partnership
in 1923 primarily as an equity trading house. Ten years
later Salim "Cy" Lewis joined Bear, Stearns from Salomon
Brothers and steered the firm into institutional bond business and arbitrage. Railroad obligations provided attractive turnaround opportunities during the Depression years.
After the war the firm moved aggressively into the equity

block trading area becoming one of the largest and most
aggressive players in the industry. It entered the mortgaged-
backed securities business in 1981 and became a primary
dealer in the United States Government securities.

Also during the past decade, Bear Stearns has expanded
in the area of investment banking (managing over 1,500
public offerings since 1982) and merchant banking. On
October 29, 1985 the firm's shares were listed on the New
York Stock Exchange in connection with its initial public
offering, and in January 1988 the firm completed its relocation to 245 Park Avenue from its previous headquarters at 55 Water Street.

Today Bear Stearns is a leading investment banking
and brokerage firm serving domestic and international
corporations, governments, and institutional investors. It
is also one of the largest dealers in fixed-income securities
(including obligations of the U.S. Government and its agencies as well as state and local municipalities). The firm's
growth and profitability are managed with great care. In
an industry characterized by profitability and mergers,
Bear Stearns' consistent growth has been generated without any outside acquisitions and, despite the contractions
of other firms resulting from October 19, 1987, this one
has imposed no employee layoffs. It maintains a trim ship
and plans to be a successful factor in the securities industry for many more years.

Milbank, Tweed, Hadley & McCloy

Predecessor firms to this famous organization date back to 1866. The present name of the partnership was assumed in 1963. The firm's name partners were all leaders in the profession: Albert G. Milbank was a well-known lawyer, particularly in New York real estate, and he maintained an active involvement in educational, charitable and welfare matters. While his practice focused on trusts and estates, Harrison Tweed played a prominent role in bar association and other professional activities. Morris Hadley's corporate practice had an international scope and involved the firm in Far East matters from the 1920's onward. John J. McCloy's career was the most celebrated, combining an unparalleled record of public service with years of substantive contributions as a practicing lawyer.

Recognized as the principal outside counsel to The Chase Manhattan Bank and the Rockefeller family, Milbank presently serves a number of the world's largest industrial, commercial and financial enterprises, several foreign governments and agencies and many prominent families, educational institutions and charitable organizations. The majority of the firm's more than 400 lawyers are based at the principal office at One Chase Manhattan Plaza in New York. Milbank also serves clients domestically through Washington, D.C. and Los Angeles offices and internationally through branches in Tokyo, Hong Kong, Singapore and London. It was the first American firm to be permitted to establish an office in Tokyo. A leader in finance and related areas of the law, Milbank has successfully embarked on a program of growth and diversification to build on its traditional strengths in order to be a creative and vigorous force in the legal world of the coming decades.

J.P. Morgan & Co. from Davis Polk

The new Morgan bulding is seen from the library of Davis Polk, its counsel of many years. One of Morgan's partners was Dwight Morrow—a lawyer and banker, father of a writer and father-in-law of a famous aviator. In l933 he wrote to his son, who was graduating from Amherst and about to enter law school,

"The world is basically divided into two camps—those who do the work and those who seek the credit. Try as best you can to align yourself with the first group because there is a lot less competition."

COUNSEL AND CLUBS

Davis Polk & Wardwell

This firm and its predecessors trace their origins to 1849 when General Zachary Taylor was in the White House and Manhattan had a population of 500,000. Allen Wardwell joined in 1898 and, as was customary, received no salary for two years. The sole telephone was in a corner booth, and, being a law clerk of less than two years' experience, he was not supposed to touch it. The filing department consisted of a series of tin boxes in which legal documents and letters were folded. Although there were two typewriters, most letters were hand-written and copied with a wet blanket on a letter press.

The principal activities of the firm were litigation, real estate title searches, and railroad organizations and reorganizations.

In 1887 the firm's long standing relationship with J.P. Morgan began. The latter asked them in 1910 to assist in the combination of the Guaranty Trust, Morton Trust, and Fifth Avenue Trust companies. An increase in capital stock was required then and again in 1912. The firm participated in the 1915 Anglo French loan of $500 million, which was arranged by J.P. Morgan & Co. and for decades remained the largest public offering of foreign securities ever made in the United States. In fact, the transaction was considered the foundation stone of the U.S. Government's case of alleged conspiracy to divide markets and control prices brought against Morgan Stanley and sixteen other investment banks in 1948 (in which Judge Harold Medina found the Antitrust Division's position to be erroneous).

Frank Polk joined Wardwell in 1920 from Washington where he had been Acting Secretary of State. At the same time John Davis was the American ambassador to the Court of St. James in London. He also joined the firm and became its managing partner in 1921.

Frank Polk concentrated on international financial problems, especially the difficulties Guaranty Trust Co. and other banking clients had in obtaining the recognition of past obligations by the governments in Prussia and Central Europe. Mexico was another trying situation, owing not only to its delinquencies on foreign obligations but its outright nationalization of properties in the early 1930s. Dwight Morrow of J.P. Morgan & Co. had become the American ambassador to Mexico and was able to provide some guidance to both sides during this difficult time.

Davis Polk & Wardwell, and its predecessors, had occupied offices at 15 Broad Street since 1891. In 1926 it was decided that the structure had to be replaced. For the next two years the firm resided at 44 Wall Street and then returned to 15 Broad for another thirty-five years!

During the 1930s the firm was busy in mopping up the aftermath of the stock market collapse and particularly the collapse of the businesses of the Swedish financier Ivar Kreuger, whose enormous frauds resulted in the economic death of two of Wall Street's most famous firms: Lee Higginson & Co. and the Guaranty Company of New York.

During the post—World War II period the firm concentrated on two new developments: the creation of pension trusts for corporate employees, which J.P. Morgan & Co. sought with dispatch, and the popular real estate sale/leaseback transactions. In 1953 the government's case of conspiracy by Morgan Stanley et al. was so successfully defended by the firm, who represented the plaintiffs, that the government did not appeal.

Davis Polk was involved with the negotiations for the transfer of ownership of the Suez Canal in 1958 and in a wide variety of other complex transactions since then. It has extended its reach to include unit trusts and other financings for several of Wall Street's leading securities firms as well as bankruptcy, public finance and oil and gas work. The firm helped to devise the counter-tender offer strategy dubbed the "double pac man" defense in the early 1980s.

Winthrop, Stimson, Putnam & Roberts

The firm dates back to 1868, when Elihu Root began his practice. Bronson Winthrop and Henry Stimson joined as associates in 1891 and became partners in 1893. The firm name became Root, Howard, Winthrop & Stimson in 1897. Root left for Washington in 1899 to become Secretary of War, and the name thereafter became Winthrop & Stimson.

By the turn of the century, the business of law was expanding so rapidly, along with the economy, that there was little perceived distinction between the lawyer and the businessman. Over half the applicants who took the bar examination in 1895 and 1896 had never attended college. As was customary, clerks were treated as apprentices and received no salary. Under the guidance of Elihu Root, Messrs. Winthrop and Stimson became seasoned in the business of general practice: corporate and municipal organizations, estate, litigation, and related activities. The firm was responsible for the organization of Continental Rubber Company, Mutual Life Insurance Company, National Sugar Refining Company, Consolidated Lithograph Company, United States Printing Company, and others.

One of the early partners of the firm advised his attorneys always to look for "a green elevator case." This meant that, when searching for a legal precedent, every effort should be made to cite a precisely identical case—matching even the color of the machinery. But Root went further in his tutoring. He told the young attorneys that "in making the court want to decide for you, you have to set up your data—financial, human interest or economic—in such a way that you prepare the mind of the judge emotionally to decide for you. And only after that preparation do you come in with legal precedents. Those who present a whole case on a purely intellectual basis do not do well in court."

In 1901 Albert Putnam joined the firm, followed a few years later by George Roberts. In 1927 these men were recognized for their success in running the firm when the organization became known as it is today—Winthrop, Stimson, Putnam & Roberts. As the firm began to concentrate on select businesses—security issues, utility financings, representation of commercial banks—the era of the generalist was ending. The days when one lawyer could handle any problem that was presented were basically over.

During the 1930s the firm represented the Irving Trust Company, which had become the statutory receiver for all New York bankruptcies. It also played a pivotal role in the reorganization of the Associated Telephone Utilities, which became General Telephone and Electronics Corporation. It filed one of the first registration statements under the

Securities and Exchange Act of 1934 and was active in the after-effects of the Public Utility Holding Act, which mandated the dissolution of major utility holding companies.

Of the many interesting cases handled by the firm over the years, few are as colorful as the "Salad Oil Case." This involved vast fraudulent transactions of Tony De Angelis, who claimed to have large quantities of salad oil in New Jersey refineries, against which he had made extensive borrowings. On the day President Kennedy was assassinated, the firm was notified by its client, the American Express Company, that one of its subsidiaries was supposed to be guarding a large amount of salad oil for a depositor, Mr. De Angelis, who had just filed for bankruptcy. The storage tanks turned out either to be filled with water, or to be empty, or not even rented to Mr. De Angelis. The concern American Express had was its reputation and the fact that its entire business depended on credit. The company would have foundered if people lost faith in its travelers' checks or its subsidiaries' banking operations. Winthrop, Stimson was therefore given the task of winning as many lawsuits as might be brought and, more importantly, of preventing any major one from commencing. Total claims were estimated to exceed American Express's net worth. Eventually a global settlement was worked out during 1963-67.

The firm has continued to represent banks, both domestic and foreign, especially during periods when their assets were frozen by various governments. It has expanded in the "new issues" market and represented Donaldson, Lufkin & Jenrette in its pioneering effort to be the first member of the New York Stock Exchange to offer its shares to the public. The firm also remains active in the complex arena of mergers and acquisitions, which requires the coordination of a fair range of specialists under increasing pressures of time and complexity.

Winthrop, Stimson, Putnam & Roberts is a democracy of partners—unusual among major firms today. The partners all have equal voting rights on matters of firm policy, and all clients are regarded as belonging to the firm and not to a particular partner. Shown (*opposite, below*) is the Gold Room, originally the main office of A.P. Giannini of the Bank of America when the latter was located at 44 Wall Street in the adjacent building. Since 1950 Winthrop Stimson has been located at 40 Wall Street, although it is now removing its offices to One Battery Park Plaza.

Sullivan & Cromwell

This firm was founded in 1879 by two partners who have been instrumental in developing the practices of lawyers specializing in business and not simply litigation. This concept of counselors with a grasp of both law and economics has been an important element in the growth of American industry. The firm has continuously treated the law as a living force that not only regulates but also advances enterprise. It has maintained a high degree of flexibility in matching creativity within the law to the changing forces of commerce.

Algernon Sydney Sullivan went into the practice of law in 1849. His early years were difficult: his wife died in the first year of their marriage, and in the depression of 1856 he was called upon to repay the notes of friends and clients which he had co-signed, an obligation that took him most of the rest of his life to fulfill. He was known for his gracious and highly principled practice of law, and he was joined in 1879 by William Nelson Cromwell, a lawyer-entrepreneur who was the archetype of a new breed crucial to the expansion of American industry. Until that time the country was one of extractive and agrarian businesses. But with the developments of Messrs. Edison, Westinghouse, and Bell, the men of mechanical and electrical inventiveness began to change America into a modern industrial society. Manpower, ideas, and natural resources were all readily available. The critical shortage was capital, and it was this opportunity—developing a new kind of legal practice to facilitate the flow of capital—that Sullivan & Cromwell was successfully able to meet.

When Sullivan died in 1887, William Cromwell steered the course, emphasizing the need to serve business clients by analyzing their financial conditions and getting to understand their total needs—a concept that may seem logical today but was pioneering a century ago.

The firm orchestrated the formation of U.S. Steel Corporation, for example, a large block of whose stock was paid to the firm as a major part of its fee. It assisted in the complex issue of debt by the Pennsylvania Railroad in 1906 to Credit Lyonnais and Banque de Paris et des Pays-Bas, under which proceeds were drawn down over an extended period. And it played a pivotal role in the formation of, and obtaining presidential approval for, the construction of the Panama Canal.

Sullivan & Cromwell moved its offices to 48 Wall Street in 1929, a space it occupied for over forty years. At this time, John Foster Dulles was the managing partner. He was a man of forbidding personality who saw the law as a dynamic force. At one point he described it as "a codification of what the community believes to be a sound and constructive way of living." He went on, "It does seek to prevent men's desires from clashing in ways that are destructive of the social order. But it should also point the way to doing what is creative and constructive. Law, particularly the so-called common law which underlies, and sometimes in practice overrides, statutory law, is flexible. It can, and should, be added to, so as constantly to open new avenues for the accomplishment of what will serve the common good."

John Foster Dulles helped draft the Charter of the United Nations, was the chief negotiator of the Japanese Peace Treaty, and served as Secretary of State under President Eisenhower.

During the 1950s Sullivan & Cromwell was an active participant in bringing overseas issuers to the United States capital markets—foreign governments and cities as well as the public international organizations, such as the World Bank, the European Coal and Steel Community, and the European Investment Bank. The firm has developed extensive expertise in the disclosure of material information about foreign issuers in domestic registration statements.

In 1970 the firm worked with the leading advocates of public ownership of securities of New York Stock Exchange member firms, acting as counsel on the first such offering and many subsequent ones. It played a principal role in creating the Securities Investor Protection Act of 1970 and has been active in the creation and amendment of a variety of federal securities laws. Its expertise in banking and investment company activities is perhaps the most extensive available anywhere.

In the areas of tax, estate and corporate reorganizations (mergers and acquisitions) the firm has developed specialist teams that are well known for their expertise and capability. Ten years into its second century the firm has 350 attorneys and four foreign offices, continuously focusing on serving its clients as creative business lawyers.

The Wall Street Club

The Luncheon Club of Wall Street opened on March 2, 1931. Among the original governors were some of Wall Street's most prominent names including: Cleveland E. Dodge, Edward C. Lynch, Hunter S. Marston, George L. Ohrstrom, Edward Allen Pierce, and Elihu Root, Jr.

The club was dedicated to the propositions that "for a man of affairs, the importance of perfect lunching facilities amid ideal surroundings with good food, well served, cannot be underestimated, and that the business man should have available luncheon facilities under comfortable and attractive conditions, contributing to his relaxation, his health, and his energy." Neither women nor men under the age of twenty-one were admitted except on Saturdays. The club occupied the twenty-sixth and twenty-seventh floors of the financial district's most prestigious building: 40 Wall Street. The club was planned architecturally as a spacious institution with every distinction which could be obtained: high ceilings so it had a maximum of light and sunshine, air and quiet plus panoramic vistas from its many windows. On the twenty-sixth floor were the main dining room and lounge and glass-enclosed sun terrace, on the twenty-seventh floor were eleven private dining rooms, capable of seating parties up to eighty, and still another open-air terrace restaurant shaded by colored awnings and surrounded by shrubs.

In January 1937 the club's name was officially changed to "The Wall Street Club." Despite the loyalty it demonstrated in the purchase of war bonds in 1943, the club received a letter of complaint from Mayor La Guardia because it was serving butter to its members.

After the war the club began to experience continually escalating rent and overhead charges. It raised its guest charges and menu prices. By 1955 the rent was $76,705 per year and the club was forced to increase its buffet price to $3.00. The board was thinking of moving, and, in 1959, when the building at One Chase Manhattan Plaza was under way, a vote was taken among the membership regarding a possible relocation. The results were ten to one in favor.

By May 1, 1962, the Wall Street Club moved into its new facilities on the fifty-ninth floor of One Chase Manhattan Plaza. The waiting list grew so long that a notice was sent out to advise prospects that the club would not be able to elect new members for a period of time. Eight years later, in October of 1972, it was decided that women should be elected as members, although it was not until 1975 that they were permitted in the main bar at lunch time.

Unfortunately, the withdrawal of eighty members belonging to one of the law firms that was moving to midtown, combined with the continuing rent problem, led the board of governors to decide that the club should not continue operating beyond May 5, 1989. These, therefore, are some of the last photographs of a lovely downtown luncheon club.

Wall Street Spires

(*Above, left*) The pyramid atop 40 Wall Street. This rich, somewhat flamboyant 66-story skyscraper was designed by Craig Severance and Yasuo Matsui and opened in 1929 as headquarters to the Bank of Manhattan Company. Later it became the headquarters of the Manufacturers Trust Company.

This building was intended to be the tallest in the world, at 927 feet. The architects did not reckon with the determination of Severance's former partner, William Van Allen, to make his Chrysler Building the world champion. The latter's 925-foot height was already publicly announced, but Van Allen withheld a secret: inside the crown he fabricated a 123 foot stainless steel spire which he pushed through at the last minute, taking the title away from Severance, who remained in second place.

Seventy Pine Street (*opposite*) and the Woolworth Building (*above, right*). These remind us that Wall Street has its due share of skyscrapers, as bold and majestic as anywhere else. Seventy Pine Street, the American International Building, was built in 1932 for the Cities Service Company by Clinton & Russell. The strong crown is best described as "Jazz Gothic." It contains one of Wall Street's best-kept secrets—an Art Deco solarium on the 66th floor. Originally this building had double-decker elevators, serving two floors at a time such as are found in the Citicorp Center. Their lack of popularity caused their removal, however.

The spire of the Woolworth Building is pure Gothic—one of the most extraordinarily successful mergers of cathedral design and a modern skyscraper. When it was opened in 1913 by President Woodrow Wilson, who threw a switch at the White House to illuminate the Broadway tower, the Woolworth Building was, as it remained for nearly twenty years, the tallest building in the world. It is a fitting headquarters for a company that has also built the largest network of retail stores.

The City Midday Club

One of Wall Street's oldest and loveliest clubs is the City Midday Club. It was founded in 1901 "to maintain and operate a luncheon club, library, reading room and other accommodations for the use and convenience of its members."

The early luncheon menus were reflective of the leisurely pace of the time and featured well over one hundred selections. There were twelve varieties of steak, five lamb and mutton-chop choices, plus lamb kidneys and lamb hash (each prepared in three ways—plain, poached with an egg or gratin), a variety of game, cheese (fifteen kinds), fruit and dessert. The average entree price was sixty-five cents. By the 1930s, the number of selections had been greatly reduced, and yet the average price of the entrees was still under a dollar.

Originally headquartered at 25 Broad Street in the Broad Exchange Building, the club relocated to a charming English Tudor-style clubhouse at 23 South William Street in 1945. It remained there until 1967, when it moved to more expansive quarters on the top floors of the new building at 140 Broadway, where it is today. The club's rooms are decorated in the Federal style, and they have magnificent harbor views (possibly the best in the area because they do not require the long trek to the top of Windows on the World). Ladies were admitted as members in the mid-1970s, and shortly thereafter they were also permitted in the Main Bar and Grill for lunch. The Drug & Chemical Club of New York, founded in 1894, was merged into the City Midday Club in January 1986.

Delmonico's

(*Opposite*) The most famous name in dining since 1827, Delmonico's has had several homes over the years. The original restaurant was at Union Square. The downtown branch has been in the Wall Street area for well over a hundred years; the building it presently occupies at 56 Beaver Street was built in 1891.

Windows on the World

(*Above*) Located on the 107th floor of No. One World Trade Center, this restaurant, which is a private club during the day, offers extraordinary views of New York. It is not unusual to look down on helicopters and private airplanes, a sight that even the best-travelled diplomat is unable to ignore. This restaurant and the Observation Deck on top of Tower No. Two have been responsible for bringing thousands of visitors south of Fourteenth Street.

The Christmas tree in the photograph, set up on the club's buffet table, may not be the tallest in the world but is most probably the highest.

The Whitehall Club

(*Above*) This famous club was established in 1910 primarily for executives in the shipping industry. It was the first large fraternity of shipping executives from around the world, whose members came from a variety of countries where there was an active international shipping business. The founders of the Whitehall Club included John D. Rockefeller, Jr. (who frequently played squash there since the Downtown Athletic Club next door had not yet been built), plus the heads of United States Lines and other shipping companies.

The club is located at 17 Battery Place in the Whitehall Building, which was built in two stages, 1904 and 1909-10. Prior to the completion of the Equitable Building, this was the largest building in New York. The club installed a fireplace with a chimney flue pushed up through the top floor to the roof. It had a gymnasium plus handball and squash courts. Its commanding views of New York Harbor were unequalled then and remain so today.

Christmas at the Vista Hotel

(*Opposite*) For many years this has been Wall Street's only hotel. It opened in 1981, nine years after the first of the World Trade Center's twin towers was completed. Pictured here is the friendly Greenhouse Restaurant, overlooking a cold and wintery plaza. Just as Windows on the World has become a popular spot for evening dining, this has become the place for lunch and weekend brunch. Downstairs, at the entrance to the Tall Ships Bar, is a fanciful Christmas tree decorated with toy boats straight out of every child's Christmas past.

Wall Streeters Celebrate the Night Off

(*Above, right*) Harry's at Hanover Square has been
an institution since 1972. Roebling's (*below, right*)
and Flutie's (*opposite*) at the South Street Seaport
are newer institutions. The Ambrose Lightship and
Water Street's office buildings can be seen outside
Flutie's, whose window also reflects the lights and
the faces of a couple dining next to us. Note the
curved shiplike bulkhead above the couple.

The Ambrose Lightship went into service in 1907
to guide vessels into the channel leading to New
York's harbor. Its namesake, John Ambrose (1838-
1899), fought for over forty years to obtain congressional endorsement for his plan to widen the
channel into New York. He finally succeeded, cut-
ting the distance into port by six miles and ena-
bling the largest vessels to enter it, thereby assuring
New York's position as the leading port city in the
world.

The Water Street Skyline from Pier Seventeen of the South Street Seaport

This section of the financial district resembles Sixth Avenue more than anything else. It all began with the building at the far left in the photograph, Fifty-five Water Street (1972). When it opened, it contained 3.68 million square feet of office space and was then the world's largest private office building. Next to this are One Financial Square (1987), until recently the headquarters of Thomson, McKinnon, Inc.; Seventy-seven Water Street (1970), designed by Emery Roth & Sons, who have brought us more waterfront structures, including Fifty-five Water Street, than any other firm; and One-twenty Wall Street (1930), a building with a powerful, wedding-cake silhouette. This was an unusually remote location for such a large building at the time, but the nearby Second and Third Avenue Elevated on Pearl Street helped.

Next appears the large octagonal-shaped Continental Center at 180 Maiden Lane. The lovely Wall Street Plaza building is next, built in 1973 and designed by I.M. Pei —one of the area's most successful designs. Behind Wall Street Plaza are J.P. Morgan's distinctive mastaba-topped office (1988) and the Art Deco American International Building (1932). The National Westminster Bank (l983) is next, followed by One Seaport Plaza (1983) headquarters of Prudential-Bache Securities Inc. and Lloyds Bank International.

Manhattan is like a poem. A poem compresses much in a small space and adds music, thus heightening its meaning. The city is like poetry: it compresses all life, all races and breeds, into a small island and adds music and the accompaniment of internal engines. . . .

New York is nothing like Paris; it is nothing like London; and it is not Spokane multiplied by sixty, or Detroit multiplied by four. It is by all odds the loftiest of cities.

E. B. White, (1949)
Here is New York

THE SOUTH STREET SEAPORT

The City of Ships

(*Above*) Sloppy Louie's and Sweet's have been popular seafood restaurants since the 1930s. In fact, prior to the opening of the South Street Seaport's Fulton Market Building in 1983, they were the only such restaurants in the area and thus have a longstanding following. Sweet's has the added distinction of being one of Thomas Edison's "first day" customers for electricity, and the only customer still doing business in the building it occupied at Two Fulton Street when the first electric customers in New York were hooked up in 1882.

(*Opposite*) The bowsprit of the *Peking* thrusts its way over the pier and practically touches the overhead FDR Drive. The *Peking* and her neighbor, the *Wavertree*, are among the South Street Seaport's principal attractions. The *Peking* was built in Hamburg in 1911. This majestic four-masted, steel-hulled ship was brought to the seaport in 1975.

The Pier Seventeen Pavilion is the Rouse Company's newest addition to the Seaport (1984). It is gigantic, playful, and a tasteful reminder of the more vernacular structures that once populated the waterfront area.

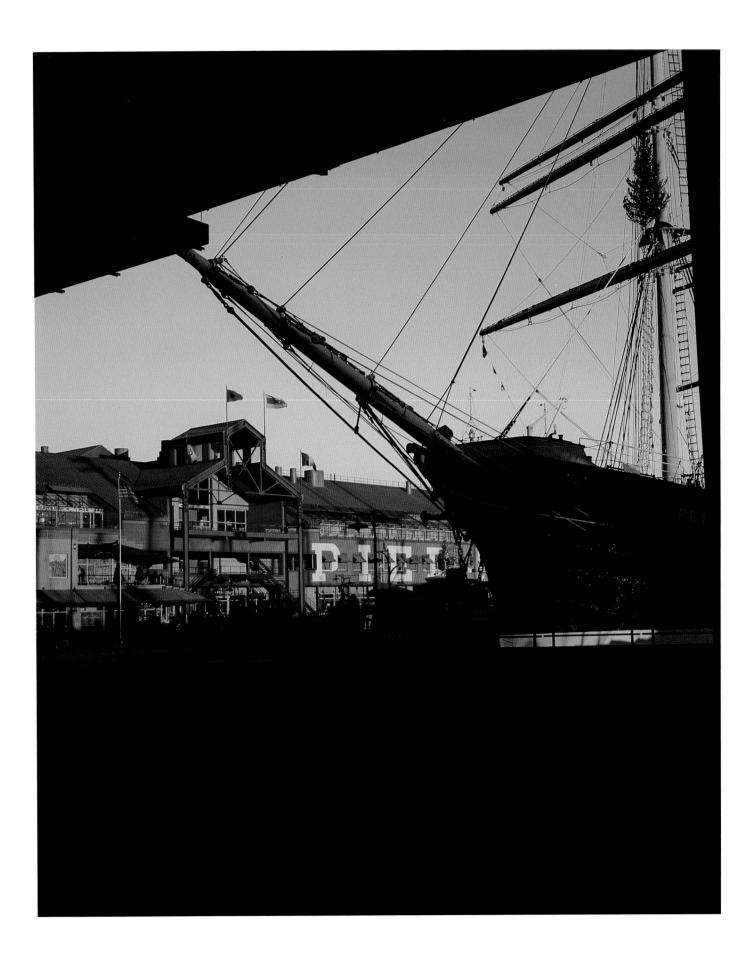

Christmas at Pier Seventeen

At Christmas, the pier is decorated with trees and lamp-post garlands. No matter how cold the weather, the water-front always draws a crowd, as it has for two hundred years.

Stretching across the horizon is Brooklyn Heights, with its piers in the foreground and famous promenade above

that. For many years the Brooklyn ferry plied this route, from Fulton Street to Fulton Street. It was immortalized by Walt Whitman, who proclaimed that views such as the one above were the "best, most effective medicine my soul has yet partaken."

South Street Seaport

(*Above*) The museum was established in 1967 through efforts of Peter Stanford. It took the first of several steps that have preserved an enclave of low-rise structures around Fulton Street (many of which date to the early 1800s). The transfer of air-rights to office buildings to the south, the purchase of Schermerhorn Row by the State of New York in 1974, and the creation of a successful festival marketplace by the Rouse Company have combined to assure a successful future for this important part of New York's past.

Without the accumulation of air-rights covering a number of blocks and their transferral to lots southward, the expansion of the Wall Street area could have quickly overwhelmed the museum area with high-rise office structures. Today, the South Street area is designated a historic district by the Landmarks Preservation Commission.

(*Opposite, top*) Late afternoon browsers pore over the offerings of the Strand Book Store, located in one of the South Street Seaport's counting houses. This structure, like its neighbor the A.A. Low Building, was probably built around 1850. In the background is the familiar *Peking*, one of the last great four-masted ships, built in Hamburg in 1911.

(*Opposite, bottom*) Holiday shoppers engaging in an old favorite pastime: browsing at Abercrombie & Fitch. Generations of children have played the games and fantasized African safaris at the old Madison Avenue store. Today the Seaport has its own version, presently the only one in New York.

The Yankee Clipper Restaurant

(*Above*) This restaurant is located at 170-176 John Street in a building completed in 1840 and designed by Town & Davis (who designed the Federal Hall National Memorial across from the New York Stock Exchange). It was originally a counting house for a successful commission merchant, Hickson Field.

The all-granite facade is rare in New York, where use of this material was often restricted to the ground floor. The utilitarian nature of the building is emphasized by the lack of ornamental decoration. The Field Building is constructed where Borling Slip once lay, filled in around 1835. The building later became a famous ship chandlery—Baker, Carver & Morrell.

Water Street, at the Seaport

(*Opposite*) The Seaport Museum's gallery is located at No. 215, a Greek Revival structure built in 1868 (note the pediment on the top and the four tiers of columns). The row of lower structures at Nos. 207-211 Water Street were built from 1835 to 1836. They house Bowne & Co., the city's oldest stationery and printing shop, the Seaport Museum's Model Shop, and its Book & Chart Store. These structures were carefully restored in 1983, opening at the same time as the Fulton Market Building around the corner.

Bowne & Co. was founded in 1775 and is now a major financial printer, located at 345 Hudson Street. The printing shop at the Seaport is a recreation of the original.

The South Street Seaport and Schermerhorn Row

The red brick buildings on the right were built between 1811 and 1812 for Peter Schermerhorn, a prosperous merchant and ship owner. They were called counting houses, with loading or storage space below and counting rooms upstairs. The high-pitched Georgian slate roofs contained hoisting mechanisms for lifting heavy cargo, and the un-

usually tall chimneys were built according to city regulations to prevent fires. These six structures were built on landfill-water lots that were 600 feet from the existing shoreline.

By 1814, the Brooklyn Ferry was landing at Peter Schermerhorn's wharf. The increase in traffic resulted in

the opening of shops, a large market, and, in 1835, the Fulton Fish Market. This area was designated a New York City landmark in 1968 and a national landmark in 1972.

In the left of the photograph are the Bogardus Building, a modified reconstruction of an earlier cast-iron warehouse, and the Fulton Market Building—both opened in 1983.

The Christmas tree is called a "Friendship Tree" and was a gift from the province of New Brunswick, Canada, to the children of New York. The Canadians also thoughtfully donated the tree at the edge of Bowling Green that appears on pages 16 and 17 of this book.

Peck Slip

(*Opposite*) This view of Peck Slip between Water and Pearl Streets shows what the lofts and warehouses dating from the mid-nineteenth century looked like before the Seaport began its restoration program.

Peck Slip is named for Benjamin Peck, who had an active ship-fitting business here in the mid-1700s. The actual slip was created in 1755. In 1763 he built the Peck Slip Market at this location, one of the many predecessors of the Fulton Market.

Consolidated Edison Company

(*Above*) On the south side of a Consolidated Edison electrical substation is Richard Haas' mural, painted in 1975 to enable a modern utility building to blend in with its historic neighbors. A view of the Brooklyn Bridge appears through the arcade, with the real bridge looming in the background.

Thomas Edison located his first electric generating station near here at 255 Pearl Street in 1882. In fact, it was the first commercial generating system for incandescent service in the country. He selected this area because the financial community was nearby (the first lights were turned on at 23 Wall Street), as were the newspapers.

Holiday Lights

The masts of the *Peking* (*above*) and the *Ambrose* Lightship (*opposite*) are decorated with Christmas trees for the holidays. The *Ambrose* (1907) was the South Street Seaport Museum's first acquisition, donated by the Coast Guard in 1967 after completing service at the entrance to New York Harbor. The *Peking* (1911) was brought to the museum in 1975, after service as a cargo ship between South Africa and Germany and later, renamed the *Arethusa*, as a training ship for British sailors. It is one of the last sailing ships built for commercial purposes.

The Christmas trees, lights, spars, and masts are a wonderful summary of the gentlest side of a Wall Street Christmas.

Winter Mist

Through the December mist appears the skyline of offices and firms that comprise the subject of this book: Wall Street. Whether seen from the Brooklyn Heights Promenade, Governors Island, or the Staten Island Ferry, it is a seascape second to none. For some, it is a collection of buildings, new and old, strung together with irregular streets. For many, it is more than that: a place to make one's livelihood and also one where fortunes are made and lost.

Wall Street Dusk

Framed by the hundred-year-old Brooklyn Bridge, here
is the greatest financial community in the world.

INDEX

Italicized page numbers refer to illustrated material.

Acknowledgements

American International Group (Philip A. Buccigrossi, Gladys Thomas, Stephan Tse), American Express Co. (Marjorie Gephart, Danielle Gespert, Stephen Krysko), American Stock Exchange (John Braddock, Sandra Lord, Patricia Moschella), Banca Commerciale Italiana (Helen Vahey), Bank of New York (Owen Brady, Michael Gilfeather, Robert Kuser), Bankers Trust Co. (Thomas Parisi, Richard Quintal), Barclays Bank (Marion Cotrone, Martin Shaw), Battery Park City Authority (Ellen Rosen), Bear, Stearns & Co. (Fabianne Gerston, Debra A. Mooney), Brown Brothers Harriman & Co. (Ronald Hill, Raphael Soifer, Lawrence Whittemore), Carr Securities Corporation (Pauline Apostolides, Charles Simmons), The Chase Manhattan Bank, N.A. (Michelle Colletta, David Driscoll, Keith McDavid, Robert M. Oliver, Sandra Ray, Fraser P. Seitel), Citibank N.A. (John Fraser), City Council of N. Y. (Michael Clendenen), New York City Art Commission (Deborah Bershad), City Midday Club (Walter D'Errico), Continental Insurance Co. (Gillian Sterling), Dai Nippon Printing Co. (Hidetoshi Gohara, Takeshi Fukunaga, Tsuyoshi Naganuma), Davis Polk & Wardwell (Dorothy Escher, Nuchine Nobari, James Phyfe), Dean Witter Reynolds Inc. (James Flynn, Beth Metzler, Miriam Nieves, Eleanor Peterkin, William Torrence, Edward Williamson), Dillon, Read & Co., Inc. (William Purcell), Donaldson, Lufkin & Jenrette (Catherine Conroy, Margize Howell, Philip Stromenger), Doremus & Co. (John Eckelberry, John Stillman, Stanley Rygor, Raymond Zipko), Dow Jones & Co. (Roger May, Melanie Kirkpatrick), Drenttel Doyle Partners (William Drenttel, Leslie Gambee, Lynn Saravis), Drexel Burnham Lambert, Inc. (Mitchel Karig), Federal Reserve Bank of New York (Richard Hoenig, John Paul Mathis), First Albany Corp. (Donald Twiss), First Boston Corporation (William Galvin, Susan Kosyka, Monica Prihoda), Globe Securities, Inc. (Edgar Crossman), Goldman, Sachs & Co. (Joan Horvich, Peter Sacerdote), India House Broad Street Club (Nicholas Batos, Gordon Williams), Ingalls & Snyder (Roger Liddell), K&L Custom Laboratories (Greg Mango), Kidder, Peabody & Co., (Maureen Bailey, Geoffrey Parker, Stewart Pinkerton), Manufacturers Hanover Trust Company (Peter Gambee, Philip Maresca, Charles McCabe, Judy Walsh), Marine Midland Bank (Robert Butcher), Merrill Lynch & Co. (Matthias Bowman, James Donahue, Lynn Holland, James Simpson, Joanne Tutschek), Milbank, Tweed, Hadley & McCloy (Donald Brant, David Siegfried), J.P. Morgan & Co. (Frederick Allen, John M. Morris), Morgan Stanley & Co. (Thomas Clephane, Peter Roche, Joanne Robinson), My Lab (Doug Nobiletti), New York Mercantile Exchange (Robert Baxter, Diana Famia), New York Stock Exchange (David Domijan, John Donachie, Charles Parnow, Edward Topple, Robert Zito), Olympia & York (Judith Dupre, Donna Smiley), PaineWebber Incorporated (John Lampe, Mary Ann Myers, Eileen Ruvan, John Wilson), Prudential-Bache Securities (Peter Costiglio, N.S. Howard, Eleanor Mascheroni), Jack Resnick & Sons (Patrick Martin), St. Peter's Church (Msgr. O'Connell), Salomon Brothers Inc. (Frederick Joseph, Aviva Ephram Maller, Elaine Ricca, Paul Ross), Shearson Lehman Hutton Inc. (Harriet Cann, Susan Manly, Mike O'Neill, Thomas Richardson), J.& W. Seligman & Co. (Fay Gambee), Silverstein Properties (John Bonner), Smith Barney, Harris Upham & Company Inc. (Robert Connor, John Leathers, Alan Shaw), South Street Seaport Museum (Randi Jo Greenberg), Spear, Leeds & Kellogg (David Nolan, Joseph Di Camillo, Peter Kellogg), Sullivan & Cromwell (William Willis), Telerate Systems Inc. (David Bock), Trinity Church (Phyllis Barr, Greg Pangburn), Tucker, Anthony & R.L. Day, Inc. (Arthur Best, Schroeder Boulton, Edwin Caplin), Twenty Exchange Place (Robert Cicciari), United Methodist Church (Rev. Warren Danskin), U.S. Lithograph Inc. (Ellen Cosgrove, Karen Quinn), U.S. Trust Company (Anne Ballek, Francis Ginnizzero, RoseAnne Pezzillo), R.P. Urfer & Co. (Richard Urfer), Wall Street Club (Friedrich Bischanka), Webster Management Corporation (Dallas Smith Main), Whitehall Club (Philip Stone), Windows on the World (Willy Blattner, Philip Romeo), Winthrop Stimpson Putnam & Roberts (Robert Anthoine, Merrell Clark, Steven Rusmisel, Robert Webster), F.W. Woolworth Co. (Joseph Carroll).